Lanes of Love

An Anthology

By:

Soulja Choc Presents

Soulja Choc

Chey

CityBoy4rmDade

Mo-Nique

&

Tosha Dodd-Dunnaville

Copyright © 2018

Soulja Choc Presents Authors

Legal Notes

Copyright © Soulja Choc Presents

This e-book is licensed for your personal enjoyment only. This e-book may not be resold or given away to other people. If you would like to share this book with another person, please purchase an addition copy for each recipient. If you're reading this book and did not purchase it, or it was not purchased for your use only, then please return it to Amazon.com and purchase your own copy. Thank you for respecting the hard and diligent work of these authors.

Synopsis

An enticing compilation of short stories from the talented authors at Soulja Choc Presents. Each story adding their own spin on Love, Sex, Relationships and Romance. This book even gives Cupid a run for his money in this Valentine's Day themed book of tales.

Table of Contents

Legal Notes   page 1

Synopsis   page 2

Running by: Chey   **page 5**

Addicted To Sex by: Soulja Choc   **page 47**

Until Death Do Us by: CityBoy4rmDade   **page 97**

For The Love Of Money by: Mo-Nique   **page 117**

Play to Win by: Tosha Dodd-Dunnaville **page 163**

Lanes of Love

Soulja Choc Presents Authors

Running

By:
Chey

Chapter One

    Taking this dreadful trip to the city already had me in a sour mood. Why did I make a promise to my family that this year I would spend the New Year with them? It's been about 5 years since I've left home and for a good reason. Living two hours away has given me the peace that I needed in my life, the peace I wanted back home for years but couldn't get. I only went back twice and each time it was to bury my nieces, other than that I stayed away. This time of the year was Esther's favorite so to help ease the empty feeling or try to fill a void I should say that my family was feeling, I packed a suitcase and locked up my home and made plans of spending two weeks with them, to celebrate a late Christmas.

See, I have a past I wanted no part of anymore, I moved away purposely to stay clear from my old life. I wanted nothing to do with the people from my past, but I know that I will be face to face soon enough with the main one that I was running from, HIM, which is who I started to refer to him as. HIM being the one who destroyed my life in more ways than one. It took me years to build myself back up and heal from that heartbreak that he caused me. While I am driving up 93N my eyes are glossed just from the thoughts of the past 5 years wanting to pack up the life I have been living now and go home.

Damon, is his name and he's someone that fits the saying when they love they love hard and his love is of the dangerous kind. It's true I never had a man that catered to me the way he did and I wanted for nothing. Our love making sessions we're out of this world, it was like our bodies were made for one another, we just fit together like a hand and in a glove. I believe he knew my body better than I did.

Leaving him was ultimately the hardest decision ever, because as I said a love like his is indeed a dangerous one. Just as much as he made me feel like no one was above me, he also made it clear to me I was his by putting his hands on me over his own insecurities. For example, he loved for me to dress up and he would show me off, but if another man's eyes lingered on me for a second to long then I would pay for it that night. To avoid an incident like that from taking place I would try to wear something less revealing, but he would demand I wear what he picked out, and I dreadfully would oblige and put on what he desired, knowing that later that night it would end with me cowerd in a corner of our room as he rained blows upon my body, making sure to avoid my face, at least most of the time.

I had to calculate and plan my way out the relationship and it took me over a year but once I got away I knew I had to stay away. Stay away

Lanes of Love

from even my family because they were close with him, my same family that I kept all those beating from. I had to stay away because the way he would look at me I knew he would have me right back wrapped around his finger. That look was a power that he has always had over me and being that I never moved on and the fact that my heart still very much so yearned for him was all bad. I have a secret that I hid from all of them, one that I know will make it impossible once revealed for my life that I have lived for the past 5 years to continue the same.

When I did come home for the funeral's I did so from a distance, no-one knew I had came. I snuck in the church and hid in the back, and would leave before it was over and return to my new life.

When I left, originally, I had no contact with anyone. It didn't take long for Damon to find someone new. I'm just hoping enough time has passed and that the bond he has with whoever she is, is strong enough that he won't bother me, even though many nights I would lay in my bed longing for his touch, I know I can't go back.

I pulled into my brother's driveway, sat in my car to gather the strength I knew I was going to need to get out and face reality and reveal a huge secret to everyone. Taking a deep breath, I got out and nudged a sleeping Jr in my back seat. That's right, my secret is when I left, it was to save my child. Had I stayed I know that it would only take one incident, one time for Damon to have a blackout and I could possibly miscarry my baby from a beating. I wasn't willing to sacrifice the life of my unborn child for the love I had for a man regardless if I had to raise my kid alone while mending a broken heart. I was already in the process of looking for a solid reason to leave and knowing I was with child was all the reason I needed.

As I went to knock on the door, it opened and although I knew I would be seeing Damon eventually during my time here, I wasn't prepared for it to be on the first day. The look on his face once he seen our son beside me sent shivers up my spine. When I tell you that our son looked like every bit of his father I mean that shit, and Damon didn't have to ask me who the little boy beside me was, he knew off rip that I had a baby from him and he never knew. His eyes turned black, his nose was flaring out and I noticed the veins popping out in his neck.

"Let me explain before you lose your cool Damon, and I hope you keep it together in front of him?" I said nodding towards Jr.

"Lose my cool, you are lucky my son is right here, and everyone is inside already, but we have all week to straighten this out and know that you will be answering to me, believe that." With venom in his voice he replied to me while stepping to the side to let us step in. He grabbed ahold of my upper arm with force and stopped me before I could enter the family room.

"You know you aren't leaving here with my son. You can go back to whatever you were doing, wherever you have been, and with whomever, but he will be staying right here with me."

"He is all I have and I'm not leaving him anywhere. Like you said we will talk later." I said as I yanked my arm from him and rushed in the room everyone was sitting in just staring at Jr.

Chapter Two

After hours of being interrogated about Jr and why would I keep him away from family but even more so his father, I couldn't do anything but say the same thing repeatedly, I don't know or I can't say why or it was hard to explain but I had my personal reasons.

If my brother had known that Damon was doing all that he was doing back then he would want to fight him, I'm his baby sister and he always protected me growing up. Every fight I had at the playground, he would be right next to me making sure it was a fair fight. The bond we have is insane but if he knew that his connect was laying hands on me a war he couldn't handle would erupt and it would all end bad. Bad for him because he was the bread winner in his family, he was the sole provider who put dinner on the table and paid the bills, bad because he didn't have the same man power as Damon and bad because no one on the East Coast had product as raw as my ex.

    Speaking up after some time passed and the questions, the subliminal remarks degrading me as a parent keeping her child from family and the father, Damon finally spoke up in my defense.

    Damon said to everyone "I let power get to my head. I thought I had Lynique right where I wanted her to always be but as we all know that wasn't the case because she got fed up and walked away, robbing me of being in my son's life." Well I thought he was going to do the honorable thing, but at least he took some of the blame.

    "Wanting your woman to respect you is no reason for you to be robbed the way she clearly has robbed you of being in your son's life baby." his bitch that was sitting next to him spoke.

    "Listen La Vida Loca unless you were a fly on the walls in my home that I shared with my son's father shut the fuck up. You want to speak up fuck it Damon let's do this, because I am tired of being a single mother. Tired of not having the answers to the questions my son asks about his dad. I'm also tired of the lie you had me living. Damon was kicking my ass for years and as soon as I sat on that toilet and seen that positive test I packed up and took what I needed from the safe to save my child no our child's life and I have zero regrets about it and I would do it all over again right now if I had to, you was so unpredictable that I wasn't risking you hitting me too hard or shoving me into a wall causing me to miscarry"

    "Womp Womp Womp bitch you had a good life, so what you got a smack here and there. You probably deserved that shit anyway." this bitch spoke up again.

This hoe is going to learn today. I lunged across the table that separated us and grabbed ahold of her long bleached blonde hair and pulled her down. We both was on the floor as I straddled her taking all my hurt and frustration out on her that I have felt over the years for him, him being Damon. I felt someone grab me and automatically thought it was my brother breaking up the altercation like he use to do at the playground, but it was Damon not Tino. Seeing him with both hands on me and grabbing me brought me back to those horrible beatings he use to put on me and I began to really flip out.

"Let me fucking go, you will never put your hands on me again!" I screamed trying to break free. As this was happening his bitch got up from the floor and got in a lick while I was off guard.

"Oh, you, weak hoe, you got to sneak and hit bitch." Still trying to break out of the bear hug Damon had me in.

"Mama why are you fighting?" just hearing Jr's voice instantly calmed me down.

"I'm sorry baby, go on and say bye to your cousins. We going home, this was a bad idea to even come here." I said with my chest heaving up and down.

"Lynique, I meant what I said when you got here, you want to run go ahead as much as I loved you then and still do I will never chase after you just as I didn't chase you 5 years ago, pussy comes a dime a dozen as you see you just fucked up one of many bitches I'm fucking, but you ain't leaving with my son."

"I'm not staying here with you and this bitch or any bitch for that matter. You want to get to know our son then you will do so without confusing him with a bunch of other woman being around, but trust me in two weeks we, me and my son, are going back home, home being our house, where you don't live and if this visit goes well we can come up with an agreement for the future with visits. I had every intention of having you meet him during my trip, just wasn't expecting it to be today."

It was then that Jr ran up to me and hugged my leg, "Mama you mean it, I can finally get to know my daddy?" then he turned toward Damon and said, "Hi, daddy. My name is Damon too but my mama calls me Jr because she said it hurts her heart to call me my daddy's name."

When he said that it broke me down. Not once did I think about how keeping him a secret and away from all his family but even more so his father would affect him. The one person I ran from, to protect him from is the very person I can see keeping him from is what hurt him the most.

"Yes son, if everything goes good then you can come back on vacations but let's not rush it just yet okay." I said bending down and giving him a kiss on his head.

"Aye listen we bout to go, me, you and my son. I'm not sure where but tonight is for me and him and I want him to be comfortable so will you be coming with us?" Damon said.

"That stops right here right now, you can't order me around I'm not yours anymore. Tell her what to do, but don't demand me to do anything." I said as I pointed to his girl who was nursing a nose bleed.

"Bitch you can leave now." She spat.

"No bitch you can. This woman is my wife and will always come before anyone." Damon said.

"Oh, she get's the wife title but never stuck around when it got tough to go through with the actual wedding, okay Damon, whatever you say. I'm gone."

I laughed but deep down inside I loved hearing that, I was in love with this man and I was beginning to think what harm could come from me spending the night with him somewhere and hell maybe even letting him have his way with my body one last time. It's been years and I have been craving his touch since the night I ran off.

Chapter Three

As I am driving, doing my all to keep calm I keep glancing at my son sitting in the back seat with wide eyes looking at the skyline of downtown Boston at night. He was amused which lets me know that he was living somewhere completely different than the city. I was planning on using little pieces like that to figure out where he lived and what kind of life he had.

"How about we stop off at GameStop and get you something to do tonight once we get back from the movies?"

"That's okay daddy, I have my tablet in my backpack. Mama says that those kinds of games at GameStop are for bigger boys and girls and I only play on it for 2 hours. I'm not 5 yet, when I turn 5 she said I can play it for an hour longer." He replied.

I had to give it to Lynique, she is a good mother. I was impressed she wasn't the kind of new age mother that has the games or TV watch the kids while they bullshit on social media. Plus, my son spoke clear and was well mannered.

"Well that is good to know. What else do you like to do Jr.?" I asked because my house really didn't have much for a kid to do. It was basically a bachelor pad.

"I play with toys, but they are all at my house. Mama can daddy read to me tonight instead of you when we go to bed. You can come too if you want?" Jr had asked looking at Lynique in the passenger side of my car.

"Yes, your dad can read you a book." Lynique answered him then turned to me. "I tell him all the time books are food for the brain and he has to feed his if he wants to be successful."

"Even though I shouldn't be thanking you because you kept him from me I appreciate the way you are raising him. I never wanted a kid to grow up like I did, not having a real childhood because of bad choices my parents made."

I never really told her about my upbringing back in Jamaica. My father was a kingpin, my birth mother I never met because she was a maid he cheated on his wife with. I heard she tried to make my mother leave, but my father wouldn't have it, but once I was born my mother was never seen again and his wife had no choice but to accept me. The thing is she never did, at least not when my father was gone. In front of him you would think she adored me but the minute he walked away came the step mother from hell. She couldn't beat me and leave marks in obvious places because my father would notice, but she put hands on me, sometimes in places she had no business touching. I was 12 when she first sucked my dick. By the time, I hit 18 and could leave on my own I did that, using coming to the States to take over my uncle's business as an excuse. I hated my mother for being a coward and not standing up taking me with her, I hated my step mother for doing things to me all those years which is why I had no respect for Lynique and treated her like shit while I had her.

What she doesn't know is when she left I began to take a long look at what I did to make her run off like she did. I guess because my step mother never leaving my father left me the impression that if I loved her and gave her the world she would always stay with me. It was immature I know now to think that good dick and expensive gifts would be enough to keep her but I learned the hard way, it took more than that to hold a real one down. I really do love her and if she is willing to come back I will try to keep my hands off her and that's my word.

I pulled into my driveway and seen that my son and Lynique both fell asleep. I guess she thought I still lived close to Boston, but I had moved to a small town in Rhode Island. I got out my car, closing the door quietly and running to unlock the front door then went back to the car opening the back door to get my son out first. I carried him into the house, up the stairs and placed him in a bed in the guest room that I was now planning on transforming into his own room. When I made it back to the car and seen Lynique was still asleep with her mouth slightly open, just like she always slept when she was exhausted, I decided to grab Jr's backpack and walk to the passenger side of the car to wake her up, so we can go inside.

"We here." Softly nudging her I said.

"Where is Jr?" she groggily said getting out the car.

"I already carried him inside and put him in a bed."

I grabbed her hand and led her inside, bypassed the whole downstairs and led her to my room. I had some things to discuss with her and what better place than the bedroom right?

"Where are you taking me Damon? I want to go sleep with Jr?"

"Not tonight you aren't, we have some making up to do, I haven't had pussy anywhere close to yours since you ran off and I know you miss this dick so we going to get reacquainted. It's going to be a long night so I hope that nap was a good one."

Lynique just looked at me, I knew she wanted it just as bad as I needed it.

Chapter Four

    The way Damon was staring into my soul was the image I had locked in my memory. I would close my eyes every chance I got and envision that look as I would use my vibrator that I searched high and low for when I was first living alone. I wanted the perfect one, as close to real as I could find, and I needed it to match +his size and complexion, so it would feel right. At first, I had bought one that I thought, what difference would the size make, but it really made a big difference, I ended up putting it down and just used my fingers because it just couldn't fulfil my fantasy. The day I came across Twin, as I called my toy I jumped for joy in the store with people looking at me crazy. I called out of work the next day and stayed in bed for hours while my son was in daycare, just pleasing myself repeatedly while I pictured Damon being the one fucking me.

Just like the night he took my virginity, in the blink of an eye, before I was aware of what was going on, my clothes were off, and I was on my back in the middle of his big luxurious bed except tonight it wasn't my first time and I knew what to expect. His face was buried in my pussy and all I could think about was how much I missed his head game. I instantly came, and I knew from the past that he had just started. It didn't take long before I felt my legs trembling as I came again, but still, he didn't let up. I tried to run due to the sensitivity that was lingering from the powerful back to back orgasms I just experienced but he had a tight grip on my waist not letting me get away. I knew the only way to get him to stop was to allow him to bring me right back and quench his thirst, so I did just that, cummin' one more time as he came up smiling and licking his lips.

"I never got that sweet taste out my mouth." He said.

He was crawling up and getting into the position where he could enter me but didn't have any protection in hand, so I placed my hand on him and said "No way am I allowing you to enter me without using a condom. I don't know who you have been laying up with, seeing as I thought you had one woman and I learned today you balance out multiple, not to mention I'm not on birth control."

"Move your hand Lynique. I strap up every time I sleep with someone, I don't even allow them to suck my dick unprotected but now that you bring it up maybe I need to. I don't know who you been laying up with all these years."

When he said that I could see the wheels turning and I didn't want this to go left and have it turn into me being hit, so I quickly answered. "I haven't been with anyone since I walked out the doors of the home we shared Damon. My focus has been on our son and I wasn't going to be bringing no man around him when his father never knew he existed."

Just by saying that I could see the tension he was feeling simmer back as he leaned down and kissed me. This kiss was different than any other kiss we have ever shared. It was like he had a point to prove. With my mind now centered around this kiss he took it upon himself to enter me, and yes raw.

"You for real huh Lynique? No one been in my pussy, this shit is just as tight as that first night. You remember that night baby. You promised me you would always be by my side, but you lied to me, you ran off and many people had to pay for that." He said getting angry.

Damon began to punish my body, but it was feeling so good. My eyes were rolling to the back of my head. I couldn't think of a response right then, but I suppose we will need to talk after this.

"I'm not letting you go Lynique. Tell me what you want from me?"

He was moving in and out but at a slow pace now, our bodies were connected but the way we were staring at one another our souls reunited after years being apart and I was in my happy place. I loved this side of Damon, he was attentive, nurturing and I knew whenever we were intimate that he loved me just as much as I loved him. He showed me with each thrust, even when he got rough, his eyes would look into mine with a softness to them, evening it out.

"I can't stay. I don't want this to confuse you, but I have a life that I love and it's no longer with you." I said as I felt a tear slip out my eye.

"Then why is your eye crying for me. You know just as much as I do that together is where we need to be."

"I used to know that but not anymore. Let's not ruin this night." I told him.

For another 15 minutes, he made love to me, then just as I was reaching my climax he pulled out and laid on his back.

"For years, I told myself when I found you I was going to hurt you, when I seen you had my son my first thought was to kill you and take him and move home to Jamaica but my love for you outweighs the anger I have and while you are here I will show you I can be the man you wanted me to be all those years ago."

"Our time here isn't enough time, let it go." I said but once I finished saying that, the same mouth that uttered those words, wrapped themselves around his dick.

Chapter Five

"So, you just going to use me for my, ah shit that feels so good baby." I just continued to lay back and let Lynique do her thing. I swear she is a dick sucking pro. I taught her just how I liked it and I can see that she hasn't forgot what to do. She can talk that we don't have enough time but I'm going to make her see in a week not two that this is home and she needs to bring that ass right on back where she belongs.

"I haven't had no real dick in years so if you thought you could just stop because I won't bow down to your commands no longer then you are crazy for real, so take advantage like I am of the moment." She said coming up for air.

This was a side of her I don't ever recall seeing. This newfound independence was turning me on and with her sucking the shit out my dick I couldn't fight it no longer and I shot the biggest nut I have had in a long time down her throat and she gladly accepted every drop while swallowing it.

She crawled her way up and positioned herself on top of me while she slowly slid down on my dick, winding her hips as she came down to the base. She placed her feet flat on the bed, bending backwards a little bit, as she put her hands on my knees and began to bounce up and down. I had the perfect view, her natural size D tits bounced, and I could see my dick disappearing in and out of her pussy. I reached up with one hand and cuffed her left tit and took my other hand and put the right amount of pressure on her clitoris. That drove her crazy and she went down and stayed down so the base of my dick was met with her pussy and she began to just wind her hips, grinding her swollen clit on my finger until she came, came hard.

"I love you Damon, I'm cummin!"

"That's right baby cum all over your dick." I said as I seen my dick covered in her juices, even running down my balls. She climbed up off me, but I had yet to cum inside my soon to be wife. If I have to kidnap her and bring her to Jamaica with my son I'm doing it. Now that I heard her say she loves me and the way her pussy was gripping my dick there was no way she was walking away from me again.

I got up off the bed and grabbed Lynique pulling her by her hair, not in a way to hurt her but in a sexual pleasing way just so she was standing on the floor with me. I bent her over and slid back inside her, I wanted to punish her for taking that good pussy from me and leaving me to deal with all this mediocre pussy for the past 5 years. I lifted my leg and put it on the bed, so I could really go in deep. I was hitting her with short deadly strokes, no need to play nice anymore, I was chasing a nut and I wanted nothing more than to bust all up in her hoping that with her not being on birth control that I would give her a late Christmas gift. If I had to trap her by keeping her barefoot and pregnant then that's what I'm bout to do, shit bitches been doing it to men for years.

I was pounding the shit out her pussy, but she was taking it and was meeting me thrust for thrust, so I stopped with the short deep strokes and began to pull almost all the way out and quickly fill her back up with my dick. I could feel my stomach tightening so I knew I was about to nut and so did Lynique because she tried to move out the way, but I held onto her waist and released every bit I had in me and I stayed inside for a minute to make sure nothing escaped.

Chapter Six

Tomorrow is Christmas, well the one my brother was planning on having with me coming to town after the holidays had passed, and once again I am spending the night at Damon's house. I have yet to spend a night with my family, but we spent the days over there. Damon just wants to spend as much time with me and Jr as possible. We haven't had sex again but every night I'm in his bed, in his arms, getting the best sleep in the world. I missed this part of him, I keep telling myself not to get too comfortable because in a few more days I will be leaving and even though I know now we will need to have contact due to our son, it will be hard. He has turned his phone off, so all his female companions weren't interrupting us, and I was surprised when none came knocking on his door, but he shut those thoughts down telling me no one knew about this house, if he spent a night with them it was back in the city.

We left Jr. yesterday for a few hours to go shopping for him, Damon wanted to set his room up and make it the room of his dreams. He even bought a ton of gifts for Jr to open on our fake holiday, which I still had to wrap for him. He will have everything he needs right here at his dad's house for future visits. Damon is still saying this is home now and we aren't leaving but I'm not caving in. I must admit his temper has been good but that also can be an act because he is trying to sucker me in.

"Lynique go ahead and take my car to the house. I have a few last-minute things to get before tomorrow and some stops to make but I will be at the house soon." Damon said to me. All I thought was I bet you had some things to buy and places to go. I know I have no right to be upset, because I was no longer his girl and I would be leaving soon so he had to line up his bitches again, but that don't mean it didn't bother me. I snatched the keys from his hand and stormed out my brother's house calling for Jr to come on.

"Aye slow it down woman. Don't snatch shit from me again, you understand me?" He spoke, and I thought welp here comes the beast. I needed that reminder of what lives inside of him, but I didn't want to feel the full wrath of it nor did I want our son to know and see that side of his father. I didn't bother to respond, I just buckled my son in the car and got in and closed the door. I adjusted the seat and then it hit me, how would he get to his house if I had his car?

I beeped the horn and he came to the driver's side window.

"How you getting to your house if I'm taking your car? Why don't I just take mine and you can have yours.?"

"You ain't running away. Take my car, your brother is driving me."

"So, you going to make my brother drive you all around doing whatever when he has a whole event to set up for tomorrow and his family to be with, when I have a perfectly safe car right there." I said pointing towards my 2016 Honda Accord that was parked where I left it a few days ago, when I first arrived.

"Just go ahead, I'm not going to be long at all you will see. Just be ready for when I get back. Have a movie picked out for us and get those pajama sets ready for us to put on and have family night."

Damon had got us all onesie pajama's even himself one. Granted his was Polo but still I couldn't wait to capture him in his. I just started his car by hitting the start button and headed for 93 south to hit the highway. I must admit, his new home, located in the historic town of Newport RI was impressive. It took me about an hour to get to the house. I told Jr to get into a bath while I went and ordered some food. Just shortly after the food came, Damon walked in with nothing in his hands which only solidified my original thought, he wasn't out making moves, he was out with his hoes. They didn't have to worry because I'll be gone in a few days and they can have him back, it did feel good to know I can shut it all down whenever I came around. What he didn't know was I wasn't that far from him, I was closer to him than both of us was to the city.

Once we ate dinner, I went to shower and get into my pajama's and Damon did the same in the other bathroom, so Jr wouldn't ask us why was we in a shower together. We gathered back in the living room and put on Beauty and The Beast, the movie not the cartoon version. I popped us some popcorn and made us some crushed ice with Kool-Aid flavor on it like a slushy. Damon and I sat next to each other, I tucked my feet underneath my butt and our son was at Damon's feet on the floor where he wanted to sit. He never made it through the whole movie so while Damon carried him to his room, I cleaned up the cups and bowls then met him back in his room.

I pulled back the comforter and slid into the bed after placing my phone on the charger, so I had a full battery to record our son's face in the morning when he realized it was Christmas all over again but this time at his dad's house. When I looked over Damon was standing at the end of the bed now in his boxers.

"Lynique, here." He said handing me a manila envelope.

"What is it?" I asked.

"Just open it please."

Doing as he asked and curious as to what it could be I was surprised to see it was a deed to the house we were currently in now in my name.

"What is this for, I told you I had a home."

"And you will be selling it or rent it if you don't want to give it up, but I meant it this is your home, our sons home. Here are my keys to it, I will leave if you really want me to and go back to the city. But I want you and my son to be in the most secured and safe house possible and this is it."

"Right go back to the city to your whores you went to see, tonight right?"

"Actually, you're wrong. This is where I went." He said walking over to his jacket and pulled out a jewelry box.

"Lynique Andrews, will you please consider spending your life with me? I will do whatever you ask, anger management included. I don't want to lose you again."

Tears were falling, and I just couldn't answer him.

Chapter Seven

    I couldn't believe that I was given this house. I was confused about what I wanted to do. I mean realistically it is a better more secure home in a better location, not to mention the school system is much better than where I have been living. I do suppose I could earn an extra income and rent out the much smaller house I owned. I know Jr will love to move because he was complaining already about having to go back to a smaller room, and he couldn't wait to come visit in the summer and go swimming in the pool, but I still ain't sure I should do this. I don't want Damon to get it in his head he can control me, I mean yes, he gave me paperwork to the house that is now in my name, along with his key but then turned around and asked me to marry him. I didn't answer him, nor accept the ring because all my fears came rushing back to me,

I left for a good reason, I kept telling myself. Just because a week has passed and I haven't had his foot up my ass doesn't mean that he is a changed man and won't snap on me once I agree.

"What if I don't want this big of a house?" I asked him.

"Do you know how dumb you sound right now Lynique?" he said looking defeated.

"Probably as dumb as I looked for being your punching bag all those nights. We have had a wonderful week, we share a beautiful son, who I am and will forever be thankful for you giving me, but I still think about all the bad stuff too." I said now sitting fully up in the bed.

"I understand what you are saying, I do, but how else will I be able to show you that this time it will be different if you don't take the chance? I know you love me still, besides when you said it the other night, I feel it Lynique, I can see it in your eyes. Don't you think you are torturing yourself by denying what it is you really want, and that is us." He said.

Damon was making a lot of valid points and I just needed to think. I didn't want to make any quick decisions that I would later regret, after all it would defeat the purpose of me running in the first place. I have my son and his innocence to take into consideration a whole lot more than what I wanted for myself.

"After tomorrow, I need for you to go stay wherever it is you had in mind for you to stay and give me some space. You being here with me is clouding my judgement. I need to make up my mind and do what is best for everyone, but us acting like we are a happy family when it can just be a temporary feeling won't help us in the long run. I don't want to feel trapped, pushed nor forced into a situation again." I told him.

"Okay, I'm going to put this ring right here, in this top dresser drawer. When you, or if you decide to accept my proposal, I want you to walk to this drawer." He said as he opened it, and placed the box with the ring and his key inside and closed it, "take the ring and key out, slide it on your finger and come to me and hand me the key and I will be all yours, but until then Lynique you can't get upset if you see or hear about me with any other woman because we aren't together, as you wish."

Hearing Damon talk about giving his time and dick to another after spending the past week with him really bothered me but I knew I had no right to be mad.

"But you didn't have to just add that bit of information. You will be away from here and me so what you would be doing I would have no way to know, just like the past 5 years I didn't know every detail of what you been up to."

"Oh, but you wrong about that Lynique. I will go stay at my condo in the city but being away from you, I didn't agree to that. I will be here at least one night out the weekend spending time with my son, unless of course you are going to let me bring him to my spot."

"That's a no. He's just getting to know you, he won't be around your hoes. It's bad enough he had to see his mother fighting one of them the same day he met his father because the bitch didn't know her place nor how watch her mouth."

"She did have some valid points, but I will never let anyone disrespect you." He said as he walked towards me after closing the drawer.

"What point did she have? That I should have sucked up the blows, deal with being hit for no reason at all? I'm worth more and I had a life inside of me I needed to protect. Her opinion nor anyone else's will ever matter to me. I did what I felt was needed to make sure I had a healthy pregnancy and safe childbirth." I informed him.

"I don't want to argue with you Lynique. Can we agree to disagree? I'm trying to work with you and do this your way. I'd cancel everyone right now, change my number and marry you tomorrow if you agreed to it. It's you that ain't hearing nor believing me so until you become mine again, I have needs to be met and they will be willing to stop, drop and roll for me. It's not like you will be around the corner for me to do a late night quick stop so someone going to have to service the beast." Damon said as he was now sitting at my feet on the bed.

"Man move!" I said now frustrated, I ain't want to hear or imagine him doing all that, and I was already vocal about it but he still carried on. Some things were better left unsaid and that was one of them. I knew I will be laying in bed every night picturing him giving that good dick away to someone else. I know Damon has a high sex drive and can't get enough so I knew 9/10 he will be with someone every night of the week who wasn't me satisfying them, while I laid in bed alone back to playing with myself.

Chapter Eight

    Lynique thought by telling me to move that she was going to be able to throw a silent tantrum and go to sleep but I had something else planned. I was going to remind her until I did leave to go stay at the condo in the city what she was in so many words allowing me to give to others. I was going to give her the best dick down in history tonight. I am relieved my son, once knocked out would sleep through an atomic bomb going off in his room so he won't be waking up to his mother's screams. She keeps bringing up how I put my hands on her in the past, and yes, I was wrong for that, so instead I was planning on punishing her with this deadly weapon that hung low.

When I didn't move right away like she demanded, she tried to kick me off, but I grabbed ahold of her left foot as she was laying on her right side, and then I took her right foot in my other hand and spread her legs. I just looked at her pussy print in the thin fabric of her panties. I leaned down and just blew at a close range on her pussy and felt her tense up, as she let out a slight moan.

"Tell me what you want me to do to you right now baby?" I said to her.

"Just do what you do baby, you know how to drive me crazy." She stuttered, as I put my mouth on the outside of her panties but covered her pearl and blew hard, letting the heat from my mouth send sensations to her, I could feel the heat radiating back from her pussy.

I let her feet go, but Lynique kept her legs spread wider than an eagle flying high above, and I planned on taking her head to a higher level than that. I took my thumb and applied just enough pressure above her clitoris while I slid the lacey material to the side and slid my finger up and down the opening of her pussy. You see, Lynique's pussy had this power behind it that some investors could use to create the worlds greatest vacuum cleaner because when my finger got to her opening it sucked my finger on in, and I went with it. As I was working my finger I gradually added another one inside then brought my face back down to her pussy. I bit lightly on her now swollen pearl. Lynique grabbed ahold of my head and pushed it into her pussy, holding it still as she grinded on my face. I was loving the way she was tasting as her pussy walls was gripping my fingers as I was stroking her with them. I removed my fingers and forced her hands from my head and stood up to remove my clothes. While I was doing that, Lynique moved her hand to her pussy and was rubbing her pussy inside of her panties, until I was close enough for her other hand to grab ahold of my dick that was standing straight at attention. She took her finger from out her pussy, and underwear and stuck it in her mouth savoring the taste of her own pussy making me jealous because I wanted to go back to enjoying the sweetness it held. I reached down and tore her tiny ass panties off that created a barrier, not wanting to take the time to have her lift up and remove them. I dove back head first to finish getting my favorite snack but this time Lynique now had her mouth wrapped around my dick causing it to grow another two inches.

    I wanted to try something new, to test her skills, that I knew she had but this was a position we never tried in the past and I wanted to see if she could handle sucking the dick while I ate her pussy at the same time. I stopped eating her pussy and moved her from my dick, as hard as it was but it was only going to be for a few seconds. I reached for her and lifted her off the bed but placed us in the 69 position while I was standing. Her pussy was calling for me, so I went back to licking and sucking on it as she once again wrapped her hands and then mouth on my dick. I guess she was loving the way I was eating her pussy as she began to wind her hips almost causing me to drop her.

    I backed my mouth from her pussy and told her watch out, so she could stop sucking my dick upside down, now thinking shit what if all her blood rushes to her head, but baby was in a zone and was going to town and I felt my knees getting weak from the sensation she was bringing to my body. Turning around where I could now fall back on the bed, I did just that then went back to eating her pussy, but this time it took nothing for her to cum and I sucked it all up.

    Don't ask me where Lynique learned the next position but it was like she got into a crab position as she stopped sucking my dick but crawled to where she positioned her pussy at the tip and eased her way down, head still bent as I felt the tip of her tongue at the base of my dick, she then grabbed my balls and popped one in her mouth. I never knew she was so flexible and could bend her body in the manner to do the impossible, had I known this I would have chased her ass down 5 years ago, when she ran off on me. It took me no longer than 4 minutes to release deep in her in this position.

Chapter Nine

    I know what Damon thought he was doing, but I had to switched it up on him. You see I been doing yoga since Jr was two months old and I was cleared by the doctors, that and when you must resort to watching porn so much you learn a whole lot. Once I felt his dick pulsating inside of me knowing he just dropped a huge amount of cum in me I knew I had to make a mental note to head to the doctors soon for birth control. I don't care what he was just telling me about once a week coming here for our son, we both knew he would be in my bed on those days and I'm going to need to get on something, that is if I wasn't already pregnant, not from tonight but from my first night back in town.

I untucked my head from the position it was in and I used my stomach muscle strength to flip my body over to where I had my body in a half handstand on the floor, my pussy open and with an easy accessible entry. I dreamed of trying this position for years and it was about to happen. I just prayed that I was strong enough to hold myself steady, but I was about to find out.

"Damn, baby what have you been studying lately, got you doing these flips and flops and landing in these positions, even I couldn't come up with. I'm about to beat this shit up like this here." Damon said while biting his bottom lip, and without warning or even going slowly he pushed all the way in and began giving me steady strokes, evenly timed and paced, but each one hitting my spot. I was fighting to hold on, but it was useless, after a dozen or so times of him hitting my weak spot I did something I haven't done in years, I squirted and due to the position, I was in it was landing on my stomach, but he didn't stop, and I couldn't take it.

"Baby, wait, I'm weak and I have to move." I said trying to regain strength because that orgasm took a lot from me.

"Nope, hold on baby, you think you can introduce me to a new position and because you busted already you can just change positions, you have to stay still let me have some fun." He said while continuously beating up my pussy.

"Bae, you have too much stamina for me to stay like this without causing my body to have Charlie horses and a migraine later, hit it from behind." I begged him, but it fell on deaf ears.

I felt another strong orgasm coming on and my body was shaking but he wasn't letting up. "Damon, baby please oh my god I can't take it baby. I'm bout to cum again, fuck baby I can't do this, I can't allow you to give my dick to anyone else. I love you I'll marry you, don't leave."

I didn't know if I really felt what I was saying or even wanted it but the way he had my body convulsing back to back to back, I was liable to admit to doing sins I never have.

"You ready for this bitch?" he hollered out as I felt his movements speed up knowing he was about to bust another one.

"Fuck me baby, give me that shit, shoot all that shit in your pussy baby, I'm about to cum right along with you again." I screamed out.

Damon slid out of me and I barely made it fully on the bed when he stopped me from laying down, he placed his hands on my hips bringing them up, the pushed my head down, put a hand on the middle of my lower back applying pressure where he created the perfect arch. I ain't going to lie, as amazing as the 3 new positions I was put in tonight was, this will always be my favorite, it allowed him to bang the tip of his dick in a place not easily found within, like a double hole as he once described and when he was in that place it was a constant orgasm not multiple back to back. It was a feeling I desired for years to feel again and just thinking how I was about to feel it again had me dripping.

What I was really wanting was him to enter and go right to that hidden place but instead he slid in slow and not fully, only putting half of his dick in and then pulling all the way out and it was driving me crazy. He knew I wanted him to fuck me and he wanted to play games, when he entered me this time I quickly backed up so that he filled me up, when I did so my ass bounced, and Damon slapped it.

"You ain't slick, you better stay in your place Lynique or you won't get what you want, I'm not ready to go there right now, let me savor the feeling of just being in you for a minute." He said breathing heavy as he was moving in and out side to side slowly.

I let him remain doing that for about two minutes before I was tired of the anticipation building, wondering when was he going to really bless me so I ignored what he said and I began really backing it up on him to the point he was now just standing still straight up and letting me fuck him by backing up on his dick, but no matter how hard I tried to get it so he entered that place I couldn't and he knew it.

"As amusing as this is and I want you to suffer baby I can't fight the urge anymore, daddy is bout to go home." He said while putting one foot up on the bed and gripping my hips tight.

At first when he said that I thought he was talking about stopping all together and going home without us making it 3 for the count for him, but once I seen that foot on the bed I already knew what he was about to do and what home he was about to visit.

"You ready? Remember you asked for it." he warned me.

Maybe I had forgot how before it got to feeling good, it was painful, but a good pain, but it still hurt nonetheless. It felt like he was rearranging my uterus when he would ram in and out of me and then POP he was in there, in that deep hole within me, and he just stopped and began to just wind his hips while being so deep inside me. I was like a faucet a child left on by accident, it was a never-ending feeling that was indescribable.

"Lynique keep cummin baby, just feeling my dick swimming in this hole filled with your warm cum is making me about to nut." He said

It didn't take long for him to release again and just fall on top of me, with his dick deep embedded in me. I collapsed on the bed and by doing so it caused him to fall from my magic spot, but he remained inside of me for a few minutes.

Chapter Ten

The next morning, I was still floating. You would think after all that we would have knocked out, nope instead we went for another round in the shower then again when we got in the bed.

I was trying to get out the bed, so I could make Lynique breakfast in bed before we had to get up and head to wake Jr up then head to her brother's house, but she felt me remove my arm from around her and she stretched.

"Where you going?" she asked groggily.

"I was going to make your nosey ass breakfast as a surprise and a thank you, but you spoiled it."

"Stay in bed, don't move and bring the cold air in, keep me warm." She said reaching to pull me back towards her. I allowed her to and she put her head back on my chest.

After a few minutes of a comfortable silence she spoke up, "Last night was amazing Damon, thank you. But I kind of made some promises I'm not so sure was the right ones to make under the circumstances."

I knew just what she was getting at and while I didn't take what she said in the heat of the moment as her word I was going to use it against her.

"Maybe if I opened up and shed some light on my childhood, something I never did before you will understand just a little bit why I was so bad to you. It wasn't you, it was me. I wasn't taught to respect a woman, nor how to love one. My father beat on my step mother and she in turn use to fuck with me and I'm not talking about hitting on me. She did things to me that wasn't appropriate."

"Are you telling me you were sexually abused by your step mother?" she asked while lifting her head to look at me with shock on her face.

"Yes, and I hated her and every other woman for it. I always said to myself if my own mother could abandon me, my step mother abuse me then how was it possible for you to love me the way you would say. I've always loved you Lynique, but I thought by controlling you and hitting on you was a form of showing love and I'm sorry for that. I see now that I wasn't showing you love, I was hurting the only woman who loved me."

"Why wouldn't you ever share this with me in the past Damon? I wouldn't have looked at you fucked up, I would have gone to therapy with you to help you let it go and not have ran off."

"About that, thank you for leaving me." I told her even taking myself by surprise.

"Huh?" she asked confused.

"Had you not left, I don't know for certain I wouldn't have had a moment and risked Jr being born by putting my hands on you, had you not taken off and me running around with all these dumb ass women I wouldn't have learned to miss you, to appreciate what I had. You did what you had to for you and our son and for that I thank you, and now I'm realizing that you taught me a valuable lesson and I won't make those same mistakes I made years ago. I want to cherish you and love you and treat you the way you deserve to be. I want to shower you with the world and make it so you never have to worry about anything ever again, not even me hurting you physically or mentally."

"Where do we go from here?" she asked with her voice cracking.

"We build and we fix what I broke, but I need you to do it. I can't do it alone. If you want to take back what you said while I was in your guts last night then I understand, and I give you my word, I will still cut the hoes off and go to the condo and let you have your space, but only if you work with me to fix our family. Put that ring on your finger Lynique and give me something to work hard for and fight my demons." I told her.

"Baby you ain't going to the city, you are staying here with me and Jr. Yes, I screamed that out because you were tearing the pussy up, as always, but only way to know if we going to make it is to jump in with both feet. But Damon, listen to me, I'm serious, if you have one slip up and even grab me with force I'm done." She warned me.

"No, revise that. I'll be grabbing you with force every night, as I hit you with those long deep strokes." I told her as my dick got hard.

"Daddy, Mommy is it time for me to have my second Christmas yet?' Jr said while walking into the bedroom, where I had left the door unlocked. I'm going to have to make sure that I start locking that bitch at night because I was just about to climb on top of his mother and make sure I planted another baby inside.

"Yes son, go on and brush your teeth and me and your mother will be right down stairs, so you can open them."

I got up and walked to the top drawer to grab some boxers and while I was in the drawer I grabbed the ring to go put it on her finger.

"Will you marry me Lynique?" I asked her again before sliding it on her finger."

"Yes, and I think I have the perfect date set already." She said while admiring the ring.

"What's that?"

"Feb. 14th "she replied.

"Sounds good to me, that gives us under two months to get everything set up." I said as I leaned over and kissed her.

Hand in hand we walked down the stairs where our overly excited son was waiting for us.

Chapter Eleven

February 14th

    I couldn't believe it; the past 6 weeks have been nothing short of amazing. I am now married to my son's father. I honestly didn't see it happening when I got in my car and took that dreadful ride to Boston to see my family and introduce everyone to Jr.

    Me and Damon was on the floor dancing to our first dance as husband and wife. I had my head rested on his chest as we swayed side to side. I knew now was the perfect time to give him the news I had just found out myself.

"Husband?" I said lifting my head up to look him in the eyes. I loved saying it and been calling him that all night.

"Yes, my beautiful wife?" he replied.

"We have another date to add to a list of them to remember?"

"Who can forget A Valentine's Day wedding date?" he said laughing.

"Not that date."

"Then what date, your birthday, Jr's birthday?" he asked me.

"No before Halloween comes we will have a date to remember."

"Okay you lost me baby." He said.

"We are pregnant." I told him.

Damon stopped dancing, looked at me to see if I was joking and when he seen I was serious he yelled out, "That's what I'm talking bout. A nigga got a new baby on the way."

Everyone watching us while we had our first dance broke out in applause.

"Baby, don't run this time." He said.

"Only direction I'm running is to you." I said.

Addicted To Sex

By

Soulja Choc

Chapter One

    I was standing in front of my bed facing my headboard when Paula called my name, I turned around and looked at her. She ran up to me, pushing me aggressively. I was shocked because I didn't even know how she got in my house. She stood over me with nothing but her panties and a bra on, I was about to ask her what the fuck was going on when she walked over and stood above me and undressed. I been thinking how I was going to get some of that pussy for the past two weeks and here she was standing in front of me naked after sneaking into my house.

She looked down at me and said, "Nigga don't say shit, just lay there and enjoy the ride."

I smiled and replied, "My lips are sealed Lil. Mama, go on and do your thing."

She unbuckled my belt and then my pants and roughly pulled my pants off me, taking the boxers along with them. In the blink of a eye she jumped on the bed and was slowly sliding down my now hard dick.

"Damn Paula" was all I could say.

Her pussy was like no other, it was like it was pulling me in further as she was sliding down, and at the same time it felt like it had a pulse beating the way it was contracting on my dick. She planted her hands on my chest to help balance her body while riding me nice and slow the same way Pinky did in one of her videos. I reached up and grabbed her big ass, squeezing it. It felt so soft and juicy as I helped guide her up and down my pole. It was like we was rocking to the same beat, our bodies in sync. The way she bit her bottom lip while looking me in my eyes had me hypnotized. A woman never had me captured the way Paula had me feeling at this moment. I couldn't let a woman take full control like that so in one swift motion, I pulled her to me and kissed her passionately. While she was lost in the kiss, I quickly flipped her over so that I was now on top.

I threw her legs onto my shoulders and began to stroke her slow but steady. She must like it fast and hard because she reached up grabbing my lower back with both her hands letting me know she wanted it harder and faster. Since she wanted it faster, I started to go faster and harder. Hitting her with some quick deep strokes. Even though that was what she wanted she realized quickly that she asked for more than she could handle. She was moaning and screaming my name, she put both her hands onto my chest, I guess to slow me down now.

I slowed down a little bit, she beat on my chest and said "No J'son don't stop keep going fast"

As I continued to go faster she yelled "Oh my God, I'm cummin' J'son."

I slid out of her and had her get on her knees in the doggy style position and before entering her again I looked at her nice big beautiful ass. It was so pretty I just had to bend down and kiss it, then I bit it, not too hard but hard enough to where she looked back at me and said, "Oh daddy I liked that."

I grabbed my dick and slid it back in her pussy while I put my hands on her hips. She started to throw her ass back at me, I felt myself about to cum, so I started to stroke her harder and harder until she began to yell my name telling me she was bout to cum again. I went as fast and hard as I could until we came together. She collapsed after that and I fell down right alongside her.

I closed my eyes thinking about how good her pussy just felt, I then opened my eyes with my hands wrapped around my dick and that's when it hit me. I just had a wet dream.

Chapter Two

"What the fuck" I yelled answering the phone as I hopped out the bed to go take a shower, this woman got a nigga having wet dreams and shit, I haven't had no wet dreams since I was doing time up north.

"Who done pissed you off?" Ben asked in a serious tone.

"You nigga" I replied.

"What the fuck you mean, me? " He asked

"You woke me up out of a bomb ass dream"

"She got your head fucked up bro, get yourself together" he said half joking, half serious.

"Ain't no bitch got my head fucked up nigga" I said but the truth was, I couldn't understand this.

"You are use to these young bitches, Paula is a grown as woman, she ain't these young bitches you use to fucking with, she like 7 years older than us my nigga."

"I'm gone call you back, let me hop in the shower. "

"Bet"

I hung the phone up and hoped my ass in the shower, I was in the shower thinking about that damn Paula, I'm gone let her know I'm feeling her and if she is playing, I'm gone go out and find me a nice piece of ass to lay up with. I washed and rinsed myself three times and hopped out the shower. I usually get up a hour from now so it's no need to go back to sleep, I decided to meditate for 30 to 45 minutes. After I was done I felt good and was ready to take on the day, I had a couple of things to do and going to the park to play basketball was one of them.

I got up and put on my white and blue Dallas Cowboys sweat-suit, which was one of my favorites, I liked the way it fit on me and it was real comfortable. I put on my gold Franco chain with the iced out cross and threw on my Michael Jordan watch, and ended it with my Air Jordan 1's. I already had my two diamond earrings in my ears, I went and checked myself out in the mirror, I was on point. I walked to my dresser put on some Michael Jordan cologne, grabbed my keys and walked out the house.

I pulled up to Denny's and parked, I got out my car and looked around for Ben and Wolf cars, we was meeting up for breakfast before we went to the park like we use to do before we went to school in high school. I seen Ben car, but I didn't see Wolf's. We was like brothers, when

I did the two years up north, my girl ran off, they promised they would take care of me as long as I didn't fuck with the girl that ran off on me. They kept their word and made sure I spent at least a hundred at store every month, real nigga shit, niggas like them are hard to find these days.

By the time me and Ben was about to order our food, Wolf showed up looking wild like he always did, he wanted people to think he was broke, but everybody knew he was paid. While most niggas spend their money on the finer things in life drawing attention to themselves, he spent that part of his money tricking on the women in his life, that's why he got it when and wherever he wanted. He sat down and smiled, we both knew he was fresh up out of some pussy, he had a look after he got some good pussy that me and Ben could tell when he got it, we wondered if his women knew the look.

We ordered our food and sat around and talked til the waiter brought out our food, we ate and sat around a little more and talked. We checked out the waitress and most of the women that came in without a man, the workers at Denny's didn't mind, we knew two of them and the other one knew us from coming here so much, not to mention we left generous tips. We got up paid for our food and left, outside we stopped at Wolf car and talked for a couple more minutes like we weren't all going to the same park. We hopped in our cars and headed to the park.

When we pulled up, Paula sisters was already doing hair on the benches, same as they did every morning except for Sunday's and when it's raining or too cold. I got out my car and spoke to Paula sisters, then I asked Paula could I holla at her, she looked at me and asked, "boy what you want?"

"Damn like that I responded."

"You know you not ready for me so why waste your time, I'm a grown ass woman."

"I'm not the average young nigga, look, let me take you out to dinner and a movie and if you still feel the same way afterwards, I'll never bother you again".

"Since you got at me like a real man would and didn't get disrespectful, I'll take you up on that offer just tell me when and where and I'll meet you, if the dinner goes well, you can follow me to my house and ill jump in the car with you to go to the movies".

"How about today at 7?"

"Not today but tomorrow is fine".

"That's cool, I'm gone give you my number, you can pick the place and I'll be there at 6".

"I like that, maybe you are different but time will tell".

I put my number in her phone, then walked off to join my boys.

Chapter Three

      I pulled up the parking lot of Fire & Ice in Anaheim a hour before I was supposed to meet Paula. She had chosen this restaurant and I had never been here. I heard they only have 3 locations in the country, two here in California and one in Boston. I got out my car. I had made a reservation for 7 but I wanted to get a feel of the place, so I came early. Once I observed what I need to peep about the place I went back out front to wait on Paula to arrive. I sat on the hood of my car and pulled out my phone just scrolling through Instagram.

About 30 minutes later, Paula had pulled in. I walked over to her car and opened her door with my hand out for her to take it, so I could help her out. I used that gesture to my advantage and assisted her in turning around in front of me, so I could take in what she was wearing. She was killing a short black sleeveless dress that fit her body like a glove. I couldn't help but to think about that dream I had and licked my lips while walking with her into the restaurant.

"Have you been here before?" Paula had asked me.

"Nah this is my first time, what bout you?" I answered her while hoping she didn't tell me it was where she always comes on dates.

"No but the girls at work always talk about it. I hope it's as good as they say it is."

I told the lady at the hostess desk that I had a reservation and she explained how things went here. We went to a open food bar with uncooked food and grabbed what we wanted along with any sauces we would want added to the food. We then went to a big circular table with a grill and a chef in the middle of it. He took our food and asked us both how we wanted it. Once we told him what it was that we wanted him to prepare for us we both just sat and watched as he cooked our dishes in front of us. Once he finished and placed our plates down in front of us I looked over at Paula.

"This spot is aight, but I would have taken you anywhere."

For the first 30-40 minutes she was a little standoffish just smiling or nodding her head. She answered questions with simple answers and I felt like she wasn't interested. Once she was on her 2nd drink going on her 3rd she began to loosen up some and the conversation began to flow better. I asked her what she did for work besides sitting at the ball court with the girls while they did hair what else did she do in her spare time.

It felt like we were only inside for a few minutes, but truth was we were there almost two hours and it was time to leave. She leaned down to finish off her drink as I paid the bill and when she wrapped her lips on the straw and began to suck up the last of her sex on the beach I thought about her lips being wrapped around my dick on a beach. I had to put my hand on my lap and adjust my hard dick before I stood up for us to leave.

Walking Paula to her car I asked her if she had a good time tonight?

"I did, and I am very impressed. You wasn't lying when you said you weren't anything like the other boys that be around."

"So, you ready for the night to end or would you want to go catch a late-night movie?"

"That sounds good, I have tomorrow off so I ain't in no rush to go home." She said.

"Well I'll follow you to your house, so you can park your car and you can hop in with me."

"Ok." She said as she unlocked her car and slid in. I closed her door and headed over to my car and got in with a big smile on my face.

Lanes of Love

Chapter Four

    I followed Paula to her house and once she parked her car, she came and got in mine. I drove to the movie theater in Norwalk with some Bryson Tiller playing on my radio. I reached over and placed my hand on her thigh and gently squeezed it before she removed my hand. I parked my car and walked over to open the door for Paula to get out. We walked in the theater hand in hand. I got us tickets to see the new Jumanji movie. We then went over to the concession area and got some popcorn to share and each of us a soda, we had just finished eating so we didn't have room for all the other things people normally get when they come to the movies. We made our way to the theater that was showing our movie and took a seat way in the back in the corner. This was my favorite place to sit whenever I came to the movies.

We were about 30 minutes in the movie and my mind just kept wondering back to that damn dream and I wondered if she was as good in real life as she was in my dream. There went my dick again springing to life. I was looking over at her juicy thighs and I couldn't help myself as I put my hand high up on her thigh. Paula had moved my hand down closer to her knee but didn't fully remove it, so I began to rub her leg with my thumb. When I first had put my hand on her leg she was tense but the more I moved my thumb I could feel her loosening up more. I slowly made my way back up to the bottom of her dress that wasn't too far from her pussy, I just needed to feel.

I am beginning to wonder if I have a problem. I think of sex all day and night. I decided to shoot my final shot and if she moved my hand again I would respect it and when we leave, and I drop her off I would just hit up one of the few bitches I was fucking. I swiftly moved my hand up her dress and was pleased when I seen she didn't have any panties on under it. My finger felt her wetness and I slid one finger in her and she moaned lightly but didn't stop me, so I continued moving it in and out. She was getting wetter, I eased another finger inside and she began to grind on my hand. I looked over at her face and her eyes was closed, her mouth was slightly opened. It didn't take long for her to cum on my hand and I brought my finger up and tasted her pussy, to my pleasant surprise she leaned over and kissed me.

"I wanna taste too." She said in a whisper.

While tonging her down she put her hand on my dick and she pulled her face away from mine and her eyes was wide.

"That's really you?" she asked me.

"You tell me your hand is on it, why don't you go in my pants and see for yourself that its real. I told you Paula I'm not a little boy and I meant that in every way."

She slid her hand down the waistband of the navy-blue Polo sweats I was wearing and into my boxers and when she confirmed that it was my dick she licked her lips and said, "I'm about to have fun with you boy."

"I told you Paula, I ain't no boy. I'm all about actions so don't talk about it, be about it baby. Let me see what you got planned in that pretty head of yours."

When the movie ended I drove her home thinking she was going to invite me in but when I pulled up to her house she just leaned over and gave me a kiss on the cheek and got out talking about she would talk to me tomorrow. She had me mad as hell, she got me thinking tonight that dream would come true, but she had just strung me along and left me sitting in my car looking at her run up to her door and go inside, turning the outside light off. I put my car in drive while thinking of who I could go see tonight to get this nut out of me.

Chapter Five

As I headed to Ginger's house I pulled out my phone and called her. She answered the phone on the 4th ring saying, "Hey baby long time since you've dialed my number what's up, where you been?"

"You know me, grinding and staying away from these suckers. Give me about 30 minutes I was on my way to your house" I responded.

"You can't do that, he's here right now." She said.

"So, you just going to tell me no?"

"Let me go find something to get into it with this nigga about so he will leave." She replied and before I could say okay she hung up.

I can't believe her punk ass just hung up in my face, she must have forgot who I was and had me confused with her lame ass man that was in her bed at the moment. It was going to take me about 25 more minutes to get to her house. Me and Ginger go back, we met because her girl was messing with one of the homies and she was the type to say she didn't date thugs, now she couldn't get enough of me. No matter what nigga she was fucking with or she had something going on with she would always drop them to get a piece of me. I stopped at a red light and put on my new Lil. Boosie CD waiting on the light to turn green.

As I drove I couldn't do anything but think about Paula and all that ass she got. She had me all pumped up like she was about to give me some pussy just to turn me down easy, now I'm on my way to punish Ginger pussy all behind Paula trying to mind fuck a young nigga. Now Ginger wasn't nothing like Paula. Paula was short with dark skin and a nice ass, Ginger was a chubby red bone with crazy sex appeal and was a cold freak. I pulled into Ginger's apartment complex and parked. I sent her a text letting her know I was coming up, so she better be ready, and her man better be gone.

I knocked on her door and she opened it with a smirk on her face, showcasing the deep dimples she had that was also pierced. "You cold, you cold. Just going to blackmail me basically into you coming here."

I walked past her, slapping her on her exposed ass cheeks and replied, "You could have said no."

"You know I can't say no to that dick so stop playing with me."

I was now sitting on her sofa and she walked over to me. I just looked towards my dick and Ginger got in position. She knew what to do, this was normal for us. She always topped me off with some killer head before anything else would take place. Ginger had skills in sucking dick as if she went to a special school for it. She wrapped her small chubby hands around it then spit the saliva she had in her mouth onto the head and used her hands to spread it all over my dick, she then wrapped her pretty lips around the head and sucked in softly. Something about the piercings she had, along with the way she utilized them to help with sucking dick drove me crazy. It didn't take long of her doing this to make me bust down her throat, but she kept going and was doing her all to keep me hard.

"Watch out Ginger." I said tapping her on her head. She lifted her head up and looked at me like I was crazy for stopping her from giving me more head.

"I don't know who you looking at like that. You must not want to feel this dick in your guts."

"You know I do but I wasn't done doing what I was doing." She said.

"You crazy, I already busted, come get on this hard dick." I said while pulling a condom out my jeans pocket that I never fully took off. I just wanted to fuck her real quick and bounce so there was no need to get all the way undressed.

Ginger stood up and turned around, so her ass was facing me, and she sat down on my dick. She was wearing some of those underwear that was crotch less making her pussy easily accessible. She slightly leaned forward and began to ride my dick like the professional she was. I took my hands and placed them on her waist and began to ram my dick into her from below.

"That's right, fuck this pussy you mothafucka!" Ginger was yelling out.

"Who fucks you the best bitch?" I asked her as she was bouncing hard as hell on me.

"You know you do, now shut up and fuck me. Go harder baby, I'm right there already." She said.

I took my hands from her waist and lifted myself up so now we were both standing, I put my hand on her head and pushed her down, so she was now holding onto the coffee table in her living room.

"You don't fucking tell me what to do. You want me to really give you this dick, be ready."

I started to hammer the hell out her pussy and no longer than 5 more minutes she was squirting all over her floor, screaming obscene words with no voice left. I continued until I filled up the condom I was wearing. I pulled it off, pulled up my pants and said thank you as I walked out the door.

Chapter Six

    As I drove to my house, I was thinking about when was it going to be the next time that I saw Paula and thinking about how bomb Ginger's head and pussy was. Damn I'm gonna have to go fuck her again soon, I shouldn't have went to her house in the first place. We be playing it too close, we almost got caught a couple of times by her jealous boyfriend. Once I even had to jump out the window and that ain't even cool. I had my gun on me and it ain't nothing scary bout me, but ain't no pussy worth killing over and that's exactly what that jealous nigga would have made me do.

I pulled up to my house and parked, hopped out the car with a little pep in my step. The old lady next door said, "J'son you must of just came from getting you some, every time you come from getting you some little coochi you have a pep in your step."

I smiled and said, "Ma you crazy." Everyone called her Ma in the hood, she was one of the coolest and down to earth older women you would ever meet.

"I'm crazy but you got to love me." She replied.

"You right bout that, good night, I'll see you in the morning." I said going into my house.

I went inside and as soon as I got in, I walked to the bathroom, took off my clothes and hopped in a shower. I took me a 30-minute shower to get the sweat and sex smell off me. Then I hopped out the shower feeling brand new. I put on some deodorant, lotioned up and put on some boxers and a slingshot and hopped in the bed. I picked my phone up and called Paula. She didn't answer so I looked through my text messages and found Cheryl conversation because I never saved her number. Before I found the text I was looking for Paula called me back.

"Is everything okay?" she asked me in a sleepy voice.

"Yeah, everything good, I was just checking on you before I went to sleep." I told her.

"I was thinking about you before I had dozed off, but goodnight and I'll talk to you tomorrow." She told me.

"Wait, Wait hold up what was you thinking about?" I said quickly before she could hang up.

"Just thinking about the night and the good time you showed me today. I really enjoyed myself."

"Me too, go on and get back to sleep and I'll talk to you in the morning." I told her.

"You too J'son." She replied before hanging up the phone.

When Paula hung up I was thinking even though I just came from having sex with Ginger I still wanted to bust one more time, I went back to look for that conversation I was searching for when Paula called me back. I had met Cheryl on Facebook, she had commented on my post and we went back and forth with one another in our inboxes for a minute before exchanging numbers. She use to tell me how freaky she was and now I was about to find out how freaky she was, if she answers her phone that is.

I sent her a text first asking her if she was awake. She texted back, "Yeah I'm up why what's up daddy?'

I texted her back, "I told you bout that daddy shit, don't start anything if you can't finish it."

"I finish everything I start" she texted back.

"Is that right? What you got on right now?" I asked her then I hit send.

"The same thing I have on every night when I go to sleep" she texted back.

"And what's that?" I asked.

"Call me on messenger and I can show you better than I can tell you." She texted.

I then went to my Facebook messenger app and clicked on it, and scrolled til' I seen her name and called her. When she answered she was asshole naked and I couldn't believe how pretty her pussy was. Her Pussy hair was shaved low into a diamond shape. She had a tattoo over her pussy that said Best You Ever Had.

Lanes of Love

She smiled and said, "I see you looking at this pretty pussy, let me see what your dick looks like."

I said, "You don't want to see this little shit."

"You talk all that shit in texts and messages, don't tell me you shy now." She said.

I sat the phone down and kept looking at that pretty ass pussy while I pulled my dick out the hole in my boxers. I picked the phone back up and put it close to my face and was watching her rub on her titties and I called her name "Cheryl."

She looked at me and said, "Oh you caught me?'

"You sure you want to see this thing?" I asked her.

"Didn't I ask?" she replied.

I switched my camera from the front to the back and she said, "Damn daddy that thing is pretty, can I put it in my mouth?"

I said "Yeah"

She reached over and pulled open a drawer to her nightstand and pulled out a long black dildo and put it in her mouth and started sucking on it making real loud slurping noises. As she was sucking on the dildo I began to stroke my dick while asking her how did it taste?

"As good as it looks. Fuck my face daddy!" she said as she was fucking her mouth with the dildo and choking on it at the same time. I told her to take it out her mouth and put it in her pussy nice and slow because I wanted to hear her moan, she rubbed it up and down the crease of her pussy before slipping it in nice and slow moaning softly.

She was moaning lightly and bit on her bottom lip, then I told her go faster and she did as I said. The faster she went the faster I went and it wasn't too much longer before she was yelling out, "Oh daddy I'm cummin' I'm fucking cummin'!"

After she came I had her slow down and we was matching each other stroke for stroke, right when I felt myself about to cum I told her to beat her pussy up and we both was going fast, I told her go faster and harder and match my speed until we came together.

Then she started laughing and said, "Thanks for the nut J'son but I'm about to go, I got to hop in the shower."

"Damn like that." I said.

She smiled and replied, "Don't act like I used you, you wanted it just as bad as I did."

I responded, "Whatever. Good night with your crazy ass."

"Good night." She said back then disconnect the video.

Chapter Seven

My phone rung, waking me up. I reached over grabbed the phone and answered it while I was putting it up to my ear saying in a sleepy voice, "Hello."

"Wake u sleepy head, I'm on my way." Paula said from the other end of the line.

"Why you calling me playing games so early in the morning woman?' I asked her.

"I ain't playing, I'm serious, so get your ass up and get ready for mama."

"You better not have me get up out this bed for nothing."

"Do I look like the type of woman that be playing game?" she asked me.

"Nah, not really." I told her.

"So, get up daddy and get ready for mama because I'm about to get in my car and head your way."

"You better stop talking like that, you getting my dick hard." I informed her.

"Well that's the plan, ain't that my job now, to always get that reaction out of you?" she stated.

"You already know but let me get my ass up, seeing as someone made some plans for us this morning and failed to let me know, but I'm not complaining." I said stretching preparing to get out my bed.

"Alright I'll be at your house in about 10 minutes." She said.

"You playing right?" I asked her.

"Hell, no I ain't playing, I'm dead ass serious." She said laughing.

"Well I'm about to unlock my door then, just come in."

"Alright but hurry up, I ain't trying to be sitting and waiting all day."

I hung up my phone and sat it back on my nightstand as I jumped out the bed. I walked to the bathroom and took a piss, flushed the toilet then went to the sink and brushed my teeth. I had already showered last night before the phone sex with Cheryl so I was just going to hop in and take 5 minutes to freshen up instead of what I did normally in the morning. I just needed to wash up real fast, more so to wake up and get whatever sweat I did during the night off. I hopped out the shower and was drying off in the bathroom. I hung the towel back up on the towel rack to dry and walked into my room all the way naked.

As soon as I walked in my room, I stopped in my tracks, Paula was right there looking at me smiling. I wasn't a shy nigga so that didn't phase me that she could see me all the way naked but I said to her, "Damn you crept up in here quiet as fuck, I didn't hear you come in the house at all."

"You better hurry up and get some clothes on before we don't make it up out this house." she said staring at my dick.

I walked towards her after she said that, she locked eyes with me until I got almost in front of her. When I got right in front of her, I looked her into her eyes, licked my lips and said, "You ain't ready for this." While grabbing my dick.

She looked down and seen my dick rising, the looked back up at me. I walked closer to her until my dick poked her in her stomach. Paula took a step back and said, "Boy you don't know what you asked for."

I took a step closer to her and responded by saying, "I know exactly what I am asking for."

She smiled and said, "You really think you ready for this don't you?" she reached down and grabbed my dick and answered the question herself, "No, I don't think you know."

I put my hand under her chin and lifted her face so she could look at me and not my dick, "So you think you can handle this?"

She laughed out loud and said "Nah, I don't think I can handle it, I know I can."

"That's what every woman say." I informed her.

"Do I look like every woman J'son?"

"Actually, you don't, but I know you can't handle all this."

"I might be a little bitch but my pussy is out this world, I'll have your young ass stalking me."

"Can't no woman have me stalking them." I told her

"You know what, I had some other plans for us today, but since you talking all this shit, I'm gonna have to prove your ass wrong."

She lightly pushed me away from her and began to take off her clothes. Once she was naked she jumped on my bed on her back and said, "The first thing you going to do is eat this pussy before we do anything."

I really wasn't the type of nigga that ate pussy but I wasn't going to miss the opportunity of getting up in that pussy, so I crawled my ass on the bed and put my head between her legs and began to eat that shit like it was my last meal. About 30 seconds in, she stopped me and told me, "No nigga do it like this." And she told me what she wanted. After I started doing it how she told me she liked it and she began to moan. The more I licked and nibbled on her pussy the louder her moans got, and the harder my dick got. She tried to run from my tongue lashing but I just went with her until she couldn't go no further because her head now hit the headboard.

I started to put my own twist to what she told me to do, and it seemed like she was looking for a way out as she was moaning louder, but she couldn't go nowhere. She started to cum real hard, I lifted my head and said, 'Who ain't ready for who?" then returned to eating her pussy.

"Nah little nigga, you ain't seen anything yet. It's my turn now." She pushed my head from between her legs and got up telling me to lay down on the bed.

I did as she told me to and laid down on the bed, she grabbed my dick, flipped her body and her pussy landed in my face at the same time her mouth was wrapped around my dick. I grabbed her big ass to control the way she was grinding on my face as she continued to suck on the tip of my dick. Then she did something with her tongue that I can't even explain but it made me let her ass go immediately and grab ahold of the bedsheet. If only you was in my body and understand how good it felt, it felt as good as they say heaven looks. I didn't want her to stop what she was doing, as soon as I closed my eyes and was lost in the warm feeling she was giving me she stopped and jumped up.

I opened my eyes and asked Paula, "Wait, what is you doing?"

She smiled and replied by saying, "Showing you that I'm that bitch, now where your condoms at?"

I looked at her and nodded my head towards my dresser and said, "the top drawer."

She opened the drawer and reached inside for the condom, she noticed all the money next to the boxes of condoms and said, "I see your young ass is getting it in more ways than one."

"I try." I responded as I looked at her big round pretty ass.

She tore open the condom and tossed the wrapper on the dresser and put the condom on my dick using her mouth. Once it was on she got up and slid down my dick nice and slow. I reached around her and grabbed her ass to pull her down on me as I tried to hit it from the bottom faster until she stopped me by putting her hands on my chest and said, "Let me do this, you just lay back and enjoy."

I through my hands in the air and replied with saying, "Whatever you say Ma."

Paula started going faster as she looked down at me and smiled. I put my hands behind my head and just looked back at her as I was doing as I was told and was enjoying the ride. Her pussy felt so good, I wanted to take the condom off so I could feel it raw, its bomb with the condom on so I could only think how good it would feel without it. She started bouncing faster, and the faster she bounced the better it felt. I had to pull my arms from behind my head and grab her ass and go with the flow. I felt my nut building up so I started fucking her from below just as fast as she was bouncing. She smacked my hand away lift off my dick a little bit but not fully and turned her body around then started back to bouncing on my dick. She bent forward putting her head near my knees and put her hands on my ankles and was just bouncing on my dick. She had the tip of my dick feeling like it was squeezing into a hole in her pussy I didn't know about. I couldn't control it any longer and told her I was about to cum as she began to move faster and we both came together.

Chapter Eight

    Damn Paula and I must have put in some work because we both knocked out last night, here she was waking me up by jumping out my bed rushing to leave so she wasn't late for work. I laid in my bed and watched as her ass bounced when she ran into my bathroom to go use it. Her spending the night wasn't planned, so she still had to get to her house to shower and get changed into her work clothes. She wasn't ready for daddy to put it on her like I did, and it lead to her falling asleep at my house. I had to laugh to myself because in reality she put it on me to keep it a hundred.

She came out the bathroom, picking her clothes up off the floor and putting them on, she leaned down and pecked me real fast on the lips and ran out my bedroom, a few seconds later I heard my front door close. I got up to go lock the door behind her and she was already gone, nowhere in sight. I went to my kitchen and poured me a glass of orange juice, gulped it down then washed the cup out before heading back to my room. Walking into my room, I heard my phone ringing on the side table playing, Juvenile's "Back Dat Ass Up." Ginger's freaky ass was the only one I had assigned to that song, so I knew it was nobody else but her calling me. I had to piss so badly, so I stopped in the bathroom to relieve my bladder. I washed my hands then walked into my room and laid across my bed just looking up at the ceiling.

Ginger had called back, I reached over and answered the phone saying, "What's up nigga."

"You already know what time it is, slide threw." Ginger said.

"Man, you tripping I just woke up and ain't even wash my balls, not to mention I was deep in some pussy last night." I told her, holding nothing back.

"I ain't trying to hear none of that J'son, slide threw, I'll be waiting." Then hung up without giving me a chance to respond. I see this is becoming a habit for her ass, just clicking in my ear.

I sat my phone on the nightstand not paying her no mind. Within a few seconds I got a notification alert. I guess she sent me a text, I reached back over for the phone to see what her crazy ass had to say. It was actually a message from Cheryl.

Cheryl: I am on my way to your house, I'll be there in 15 minutes, I need to feel the real thing.

Me: Stop playing you don't even know where I lay my head at.

I never told her any private details about me, she was just a bitch I met off the internet.

Cheryl: I'm dead ass serious. Give me 15 minutes and you will see when I am at the door. When you want something bad enough you get the information you need to make it happen.

Me: Alright, where I live at then if you think you know.

Cheryl: You stay on the east side 2200 Croesus Ave in a blue house

I jumped up thinking how the fuck she know where I stay at, then jumped up to run into the shower to wash last night's sex off of me. I took a quick shower just paying attention to my face, dick and pits. I hopped out the shower, grabbed a towel and wrapped it around me as I pulled the sheets and pillow cases from my bed and tossed them in the washer. I grabbed a clean set from the closet and made up the bed. As soon as I finished my doorbell had rang.

I walked to the door and looked out and it was really her standing on the other side, with her hand on her hip. I unlocked my door and pulled it open wearing nothing but the towel I put on after I came from the shower. When I opened it, she stepped in wearing a mid-thigh white leather coat with a Green Bay beanie on her head, with some open toed white stilettos. She had her toes painted green and yellow to represent her favorite NFL team. I liked to see a woman who took the time out to match. As soon as she was all the way in the house, I closed and locked the door then turned towards her.

She smiled and said, "Oh, I see you paid attention to my text message and listened. You know what I came here for and you nice and ready." As she licked her lips adding a dramatic touch to it.

"Cheryl, I see your ass is crazy. How the fuck you get my address for real." I asked her.

She pushed me up against my door and snatched the towel off me. My dick was still soft, but I wasn't trippin I knew that I was working with a little something and it still had hang time.

"It looks like you need a little help." She said while smiling. Right after she made that comment she untied the belt to the jacket and let it drop to the floor revealing she had nothing at all on. This crazy girl drove all the way over here naked, she lucky her ass ain't get pulled over for speeding or some shit, but as bad as she was looking, I'm sure the cop would have let her go with a warning.

Once the jacket was fully on the floor and I took in her body from head to toe in person, my dick instantly bricked up. She bit her bottom lip then said, "Now that's what I'm talking about." Dropping to her knees as she said it.

Cheryl grabbed my dick with her left hand, and she blew on the tip of my dick before kissing it softly. She put the head in between her lips and licked around the base of my mushroom shaped head. She took her lips off it fully then blew on it again, and proceeded to repeat the steps a few times, she was driving me fucking crazy. I wanted to grab her head and shove my dick in her above average wet mouth. She then grabbed my dick with both hands and did some shit I can't even describe that felt like magic. It caused my knees to almost buckle and I had to grab the door knob handle to keep my composure. I regained control of my legs so that she wouldn't know that she had that control. She was a pro, she just had started sucking on my dick and already had my head going crazy fighting the urge to cum so soon. I refused for her to have that power over me and gain some bragging rights, so I pushed her head away.

"Let's go to my room." I told her buying time.

"No, I want it right here and right now." She told me as she leaned over and pulled out a golden Magnum from her jacket pocket. She really came prepared and brought the right size shit. I couldn't use them free clinic shits.

She opened it and slid it on my dick. I reached down and picked her up in the air, she grabbed ahold of my dick and helped position it at her opening. As I eased into her pussy I was surprised to see how tight she was. I had one of her legs in each arm and she grabbed ahold of my shoulders, she then took control and began to bounce up and down as she was up in the air, with me assisting her by lifting. As she was bouncing, I began to take steps towards my bedroom. I liked the way she was trying to take control and help me. Each step I took I lifted my arms to lift her up and she assisted me by bringing her ass back down.

I laid her on my bed carefully to make sure my dick didn't fall out. I placed her legs on my shoulders and cuffed my arms under each of her shoulders. I was leaned in close to her looking her in her eyes as I stroked her nice and slow, keeping a steady pace. Looking into her eyes did something to her that made a whole other sex drive within her come alive. She reached for my lower back, pulling me further into her but I continued hitting her with the same slow strokes I started with once I laid her on the bed. I put every inch of my dick in her and started to vibrate in her as she started to cum real hard, I could feel all that pressure trying to push my dick out her.

I waited until she finished cummin' then I picked up my speed and was hitting her g-spot harder and faster.

"Yeah, Daddy, that's what I'm talking about, this is what I came here for. Fuck this pussy!" she said while moaning.

I could tell by the look she was giving me that she liked the way I was stroking her, so I stepped it up another notch and began fucking the shit out of her. The way she was moaning and trying to run from it I could tell she was feeling both pleasure and pain from my deadly quick long strokes. She was loving the combination of feelings I was bringing to her. I felt myself about to cum, so I slid out of her.

    I stood up and pulled her to the edge of the bed. I took my hands and guided her to turn around and create the perfect arch I wanted before I entered her in the doggy style position. That arch gave me the perfect view of her ass, so I could see my dick disappear as I once again began to fuck her nice and slow. Cheryl wasn't feeling that, she began to back her ass up on me, so I went faster and faster and just when she thought I couldn't go any faster I felt my nut about to come I grabbed her by her beanie and began to bang her as hard and fast as I could, all my inches was deep in her, she was trying to run. I was pulling the beanie with force trying to stop her from running and it came off, I tossed it on the floor and grabbed ahold of her hair instead with one hand while smacking her ass real hard with the other. I looked down at my dick and seen it coated with her cum. After a few more pumps I filled up the condom as I came hard as fuck.

    I pulled out of her and Cheryl collapsed onto my bed breathing hard on her stomach. I leaned over and smacked her ass one more time real hard, she jumped and turned onto her side and looked up at me and said. "I liked that, I ain't even going to lie J'son, your dick game is the truth."

Chapter Nine

    Cheryl had left from here about 30 minutes after we had ourselves another round. She wasn't walking out the door with the same confidence she had when she strolled her ass in this bitch. She must have thought she was going to come get a young nigga sprung off her shit and it ended up being the other way around. I ain't going to lie, she had some fire head and her pussy was grade A. It was some of the best new pussy I have had in a long time. I'm known for dipping in some random pussy all the time but most times it be some of those no wall having hoes that's a waste of time. Whenever I come across a bitch with that good shit, where every time those walls contract I can feel it I try to keep that around. I think Cheryl is about to be one of the few bitches I break off on a regular, unless she gets too clingy. I wasn't checking for no steady bitch, unless it was Paula of course.

I was laid back on my white leather sectional, one leg was resting on the ottoman while one foot was planted on the floor. I was flipping through channels looking for something to watch until later tonight. Ben and Wolf and I had made plans to hit up Synn and see something shake. Synn was a popular strip club over on N. La Cienega Blvd that we would go to, looking for a bad bitch to take home. The hoes up in there was always willing to get a taste of this dick. Let's just say I was known for breaking backs, but not breaking bread but they was cool with that.

Giving up on finding something good enough to grab and keep my attention I put on the movie Belly and picked up my phone. I have seen the movie enough that I could hear what was being said and know what was going on, therefore giving me room to multitask and fuck with some bitches online. I put my remote down next to me and picked up my iPhone 8 plus and just as I unlocked it I received a text message from Cheryl that made me laugh.

Cheryl: J'son I should have known from our video session that fucking you would be crazy, so why did I set myself up the way I did and go over your house to feel the real thing and test you out to see if your dick game would be as good as you made it appear?

Me: I'm real gutta with it ain't I? What's wrong you need more already?

I texted her back inserting an old pic I had in my phone of my dick with precum on the tip and included the laughing emoji.

Cheryl: I am doing the opposite. As tempting as it is to turn around and come back and bust it open for you that will be all bad. I'm not going to front your dick can be molded and make millions

Me: You're crazy Cheryl but even if I did have my dick cloned, can't no silicone put in the work like I can. It takes more than the dick itself to do what I do, bitches need me behind it

Cheryl: You are so cocky J'son

Me: I know I am, ain't we already agreed on that when I banged your tight little pussy up today.

Cheryl: Any way thanks for letting me test ride it but I'm not going to be attempting to purchase it. That dick will fuck my entire world up and I can't be running around crazy behind a man so I'm going to be staying away from you and putting you on my block list, I just wanted to explain my reasons before I did it.

Me: Aight but it will be you losing out on this dick, pussy comes a dime a dozen to me

When I hit send, I got a text back with an automatic message letting me know that she wasn't accepting messages from me at this time. I couldn't believe after one time she was willing to give up getting it again. This was something that I never had happen to me before, so I was going to hit the phone button to call her phone to see was she serious and if it went right to voicemail, but I wasn't going to go that far and leave her ass alone. If she ain't want the dick no more then like I said in the text she didn't get it will be her loss, but damn I sure did want to tap that ass a few more times. Oh well, I'll find another bitch to fuck on if I had to, I had many lined up waiting on my call anyway.

I exited out the text message and just shook my head. I went to the Facebook app and clicked on it to see what bullshit everyone was posting today. I swear mothafuckas be on her stunting like they live a life they know nothing about forgetting folks know them in real life. If I didn't use this shit as another way to meet hoes I would do away with it. I swear almost everyone on my newsfeed was an upcoming rapper with 100 mix CDs out but hasn't been discovered yet and was broke living at their mama's house or they was posting those get rich quick posts talking bout it really works I made this amount last week, yet just a week ago I seen them walking out the LQ store with a $1.00 can of Natural Ice bumming a smoke from a passerby. I guess Ginger seen my name turn green on messenger and that I was online because my phone rung. I ignored the call and was about to log off Facebook when the phone rang right back.

"If I ain't pick up the first time why would you call me right back, I'm busy Ginger." I told her.

"Why you ain't come over when I told you to earlier. I was waiting for you for hours and now my boring ass man is on his way here." She said with a little bit too much attitude for my liking.

"I didn't come because I didn't agree to that shit, that's on you. Your nigga will be there soon, suck his dick."

"I don't get why you treat me so fucked up J'son." Ginger said changing the tone in her voice. I guess she realized I wasn't feeling the way she was speaking to me.

"Ginger you ain't my bitch for one, I never made any promises to you other than to fuck you here and there when I wanted to."

Now crying she said, "You know how I feel about you J'son. I'll leave my nigga right when he walks in this door all you have to say is the word and it's done, and I'll be all yours."

"You will be a dumb ass bitch if you cut off your money supply because I ain't never going to commit to you and try to take that niggas place."

"I'm not asking you to do what he does, I just want to be with you." She said still crying.

"That will never happen, I don't look at you in that way, you just a piece of good pussy Ginger, if you can't deal with the program as it has been then let me know now and I'll block your ass and never call you when my dick wants some." I said not feeling even a little bit sorry.

Ginger knew what it was, she was a challenge at first, she said she would never fuck with or be with a nigga like me, now here she is shedding tears because she couldn't have me.

"Tell me what you want me to do and it's done." She said.

"Leave me alone, you crazy and I see you going to turn out to be a problem. It was fun while it lasted but your time is up." I told her and hung up the phone.

I went to her contact and blocked her, also made a mental note to block her on social media when I did go back on, so she had no way of contacting me. Then I realized, just that fast I was down two good pieces of ass, Cheryl and now Ginger. I know one thing Paula's ass wasn't going anywhere, now that was some pussy I would not walk away from or let her get away.

Me: How is work going beautiful?

Paula: Same as it goes every day, except today is dragging more because I am tired from last night.

Me: Is that right?"

Paula: And you know it (smile face emoji next to the blowing kisses one)

Me: I have something nice and flavorful for you to kiss.

Paula: In your words, is that right? (side eye emoji) Well let me get back to chasing this money I'll hit you up after work if that's okay.

Me: If you know what's good for you, you will check in with your new daddy (laughing emoji) but I'm not really laughing Paula, I already told you, you gonna be mine.

I sat my phone down at this point and closed my eyes deciding I needed to take me a pow wow nap before tonight. I woke up about 2 hours later, got me a good stretch in then put my hand in my pants to fix my hard dick. It don't matter how much pussy I get or what the circumstance was I always woke up hard as hell. I got up and walked into my room and remembered I left my phone in the living room, so I back tracked to grab it, so I could get some food delivered, a nigga was hungry as fuck.

***

The one thing that sucked about Synn's was we didn't have no pull with security, so we couldn't just walk in by them without being searched. As I was being patted down one of the main strippers was walking by and stopped.

"Tony, you be careful where you pat that one at, he has a concealed weapon on him at all times that can't be removed." She said laughing.

"Bridgett, you crazy, but how you doing baby?" I said now cleared to enter all the way. I walked up to her and planted a kiss on her cheek.

"I'll be feeling great if you tell me you are taking me home with you tonight, it's been way too long since this pussy here has gotten the right kind of pounding she needs." She said back to me.

"Nah, I ain't trying to have no smoke with Biggs. A nigga ain't scared but you spoken for and we all know that nigga will bust first and ask questions later. I'm not trying to break up anyone's marriage for laying this pipe. I'm surprised you still working here taking your clothes off now that you got married."

"That's cause pussy is power, and I run shit."

"You might got some fire pussy but I'd never let a bitch run the show in my marriage."

"I guess you ain't met your challenge yet." She yelled as she walked away, heading towards the V.I.P. section.

Me, Ben and Wolf made our way to the station to exchange our hundreds for ones getting ready to make it rain on some of the baddest bitches up in here. This wasn't our first time up in here, and we was known to shower these hoes, and they loved it. We always left with a bitch or two each for a long night of fun. Once we each got our money we went over to V.I.P. and sat at the assigned table for us and signaled for our bottle lady to come over. She walked up wearing nothing but some string that really didn't cover much but her nipples and the slit to her pussy. Baby was beautiful, a bad ass Latina. She had some long ass hair pulled up into a high ponytail and I could tell she used some glittery lotion all over her body because it was glistening off the lights. When she opened her pretty pink lips to speak I was stuck looking at how perfect and pretty her teeth were. These niggas started pushing on me clowning the way I was looking at shorty.

"What can I start y'all off with, you automatically get a bottle of your choice, top shelf of course for reserving this section, along with three different chasers?" she told us. I never seen her here before, so she didn't know we knew what the deal was.

"Bring a bottle of Hennessy Pure White with some red bulls, cranberry juice and orange juice oh and add a bottle of Cîroc and Patron to that" I told her as I handed her $250 for the extra bottles and told her keep the change and winked.

"Oh, you just showing out tonight, big spender over here." Ben said laughing.

"That nigga J'son just trying to impress the hoe so he can add her to his list." Wolf added.

"If only you niggas knew what was going on with ya homie the past 48 hours." I replied.

"Spill it then, shit we don't read minds we blow em." Ben said.

"Man, a nigga been busy, I hooked up with Ginger again the other night after I took Paula out, came home from her crib and this shorty Cheryl tried to call me out so I ended up mind fucking her over video chat. Next day, Paula comes over to chill, she had some plans for us that fell through because shit went down for real with me and her bad ass, we woke up this morning, she left out and here go Cheryl poppin' up at the crib, so I broke her off. I ain't gonna lie she had some good ass pussy. Next thing I know, Ginger having a fit because I didn't go fuck her, Cheryl hit me up after she left canceling my ass cause she scared of being attached to the dick. Man, I lost two good pieces off ass in 30 minutes but what I gained was better than both Ginger and Cheryl together."

"So basically, what you just told us is that you finally got some ass from Paula and at the same time you lost two hoes but them hoes together ain't as good as the shit you got from Paula?" Ben asked me.

"If you only knew my nigga." I said

"Ah, is this the same J'son I went to school with sitting her telling us this shit?" Wolf said starting to clown like his ass always did.

"It sure do look like that nigga and I thought when that bitch walked over here a minute ago with our bottles and he was eye fucking her that it was our nigga J'son the playa but I'm not so sure anymore, it sound like homie in love, talking about he lost two but what he gained was better, so basically he saying she fucked the shit out his as." Ben said joining in on let's talk shit to J'son repeating what he already had asked me.

"Shut the fuck up, both you niggas sound dumb, ain't no bitch fucked me and made me they bitch."

"Who said you was Paula's bitch? I ain't say that shit and neither did Wolf but you have to admit shit sounds funny coming out your mouth." Wolf replied.

"Well if you knew what I knew and you was in my skin last night you wouldn't be sitting her talking shit."

"Nah, I'm fucking with you bro, she is bad as fuck and if it was me and she had that cut the blood circulation to my dick I'd be feeling the same way." Ben said.

"I ain't say she did all that, you going over board, ain't no bitch here, she just had some tricks I wasn't expecting that's all, she ran out the crib with a slight limp this morning."

"I feel you my nigga, get that and lock that shit down, I know I would." Wolf said and gave me dap.

For the rest of the night, we had a good time, dropped a few stacks on these bitches, chopped it up then left. For once I left alone, not wanting to really do anything but go home get undressed and send a good night text to Paula.

Chapter Ten

  I walked in the house, went and sat on the couch and picked up the remote control. I logged into my YouTube account on my T.V. app and went to the suggestions playlist. I was watching the new Kevin Gates video. Halfway thru the video my phone vibrated, I pulled it out my pocket and seen it was Paula calling so I answered it.

  "Hey beautiful." I said.

  "Hey you. I'm getting off work in about 2 hours, I was wondering if you wanted to meet me at TGIF for dinner?" she asked me.

"Yeah, I'll be there." I told her.

"Okay so does 7 p.m. sound good for you?" she answered.

"Yeah, that's perfect." I responded.

"Okay, I have to get back to work, I'll be seeing you at 7 then.". She said.

I sat my phone down on the coffee table and went back to watching music videos for another 30 minutes. I got up and went to my bedroom, I walked to my closet to look for something to wear. I pulled out some dark blue Levi's and a plain white shirt. I laid everything on my bed. I pulled my shirt off, then stepped out my jeans and headed for the bathroom to hop in a shower.

Stepping out the shower, I went in the room and walked to my dresser, got out some boxers and socks because I forgot to do that before. I put them on, then added lotion to the key spots on my body, put some deodorant on and walked to my bed. I put on my outfit then sprayed on my favorite Joop cologne. I looked myself over and as always was pleased. I looked clean with a simple look tonight, but I still looked good as fuck.

I went back to the living room to finish watching videos until it was time for me to leave and go meet Paula, I looked at my phone and seen the time said 6:30 so I turned the tv off and left out the door to go meet up with her. I got in my car and was in a relaxed state of mind until I pulled up to TGIF's and parked. I got there a little earlier than she had asked me to, so I got out the car and went inside so that I could get us a table and be sitting down waiting for her when she gets here. She worked all day and didn't need to be standing around and waiting, I figured. No sooner did I get seated my phone vibrated and it was Paula calling me.

I answered the phone, "Hey Ma."

"Hey, I'm parking my car next to yours, but I don't see you inside it."

"I came on in and got us a table I was just seated." I informed her.

"Good, I'll be right in. I'm getting out my car now." She said.

"Okay, see you in a second." I replied then hung up the phone.

When she walked in and was visible I stood up and gave her a hug and kiss on her cheek as she blushed. I pulled her chair out for her to sit down, waited until she was comfortable and then went back around to take my seat again. We just smiled at each other for a minute then I said, "Ma, what you waiting on you ain't going to order your food."

"Daddy I was waiting on you, you take the lead." She said.

I licked my lips and said, "Don't start anything you can't finish right now."

Paula giggled and responded, "Boy what are you talking about I finish everything I start this ain't the time or the place?"

We looked thru the menu until we found what we wanted to order, and the waitress walked over and wrote it down then walked away to put it in.

Looking at me with a serious look on her face Paula took a sip of the water that we each got and said, "J'son what do you want with me?"

She threw me off guard with that, so I asked her, "What do you mean by that?"

"I'm asking what you want from me because I'm not one of these little girls you around here fucking on all the time. I did some research and I know you get around and the little thots are fine with you being that playa you are as long as you give them attention here and there they fine with how you live, you have a pattern but you need to know that I'm no little girl and I won't be one of a dozen you are fucking around with so it's either that lifestyle you been living or its we see where this can go with us."

"If you ready to take me serious I'll give up all that shit for you."

"Again J'son, I'm not one of these little girls, I wouldn't have given you this pussy if I didn't want that eventually. I wouldn't have been at your house that night and nothing would have took place."

"I know you're nothing like the rest of these hoes that's what made me want you. I never been with just one female before but if you willing to take it there then I'm willing to give it a try" I informed her.

"As long as you ain't with the games then we can give it a try but if you are don't waste my time or yours." Paula said.

"One thing about me is I don't play games Ma. I say what I do and do what I say. I may not know what its like to be with just one female, but I really want to go there with you. I just ain't want to waste my time with these little girls and was waiting to find a woman." I told her.

"Well if you willing to give it a try then we can do that. Just like you never been with a older woman, I've never been with a younger man, so this could be a learning experience for the both of us. So, let's do it." she responded.

We talked going back and forth getting to know one another. Once the food was brought over to us, silence took over as we began to eat. I dug my fork into my potatoes and fed her some making sure I left a little on her lips when I pulled my fork away, just so I could see her lick her lips. She picked up some food off her plate and fed it to me, while looking in my eyes. There was an older couple sitting at the table next to us and they looked over at us and smiled seeing me and Paula feeding one another, having a good time.

We finished eating, I paid for the food and left a tip. We walked out of Friday's with my arm wrapped around her waist. When we got to our cars, we shared a brief kiss.

"Are you going to follow me to my spot?" she asked me.

"I'll follow you to hell if that's where you were headed." I said.

I hopped in my car and followed Paula to her house. We sat on her couch and watched Love and Basketball. By the time the movie was over we was getting sleepy, Paula got up and pulled me up and led the way to her room. I stripped down to my boxers and she stripped down to her panties and we climbed in her bed. We laid down and got comfortable and just cuddled until we fell asleep.

Lanes of Love

Soulja Choc Presents Authors

Until Death Do Us

By

CityBoy4rmDade

"Never in a million years could I have imagined meeting a woman as altruistic as you, Fatimah. Allah in his infinite wisdom knew that I needed a pious and virtuous Muslima by my side!" Rafique announced as he recited his vows.

Rafique stood nose to nose with his bride adorned in an elegantly customized Tom Ford Tuxedo. Fatimah had hand selected the tuxedo merely a week after she and Rafique had gone on their first cyber date as a result of Fatimah being a native of Luanda, Africa. Fatimah was born into the Islamic faith and prided herself on virtues.

Rafique continued, "Three years ago, when I met you on Facebook, you inspired me to succeed from thousands of miles away. You confided in me, but little did you know... I was just on the social site to wish my family and distant friends a farewell because I had planned on committing suicide."

The ceremonial attendees gasped at his revelation. He locked eyes with his foster mother as she sat in the first pew of the mosque. The mosque occupied a hundred of Rafique's friends, family, and associates, but Rafique inhaled deeply, exhaled, and continued to speak, "At that time in my life, I was dealing with so many demons... I had just gotten my bachelor's in sociology and was the most popular bachelor on the college campus. I had everything I could ever hope for at the age of twenty-two, but that same day, my doctor confirmed that I had also contracted the HIV virus."

Rafique was ashamed; it was the first time that he had openly revealed this to anyone outside of Fatimah.

"But then you introduced me to Islam, and I learned who Allah was, and at that point, I gained so much confidence and security from knowing that my life and wellbeing was in the hands of such a remarkable God and that nothing could claim my life or my sanity unless it was in Allah's will. You taught me that, Fatimah, and you also accepted me. You really saved my life, and for that, I vow to be always faithful and loyal to you. I vow to always protect you, and I vow to stay on the path of Allah as he directs our lives..."

Fatimah gracefully stood and patiently absorbed the words of her fiancé.

Fatimah being a native of Africa and as a Muslim from birth opted to sport a tailor made Vera Wang dress complete with a Vera Wang hijab covering her hair. She wore opened toed Vera Wang pumps and refrained from applying any make up, preferring to show her natural beauty, and a beauty she was. Fatimah stood at about 5'6 and 140 pounds. Her frame was firm and slightly athletic. At twenty-eight-years-old, she had the appearance of a woman barely eighteen.

"Thank you, honey," she responded in her thick, African accent. This was the first time she had stood next to the man that had rescued her from the iron fisted African democracy.

"Wow, I am speechless, Rafique. I have never had a man, or anybody for that matter, show me the love and loyalty that you have, and even from thousands of miles away, you have impacted my life tremendously. Your heart is so pure and transparent! Years ago, as a young girl, I always dreamed of being the perfect wife, and you have allowed that dream to now become my reality. Standing before Allah, I vow to be your support. I vow to be a great listener, and I vow to cater to your every need. I have also suffered what I thought would prove to be my demise, but I have persevered in the midst of utter chaos, so thank you. Thank you for being an ear when I needed it most, and thank you for reaching a hand out to help me. You are amazing!"

As the vows ended and the ceremony continued, Rafique and Fatimah swayed in each other's arms to the rhythms of classical jazz. Islamically, music is prohibited under most circumstances outside of ceremonial purposes, and Fatimah enjoyed the rare occasion to sooth her anxiety in the arms of the man she had just married.

"I am so happy for you," Rafique's foster mother greeted before whispering in his ear... "Honesty is always the best policy. I admire your courage, but your past is a reality, and no matter how hard you try to cover it up, it remains a part of you," she warned before sauntering off.

Rafique was slightly flabbergasted by his foster mother's blunt warning.

"Rafique, honey, is everything alright?" Fatimah inquired after feeling the slight tension in the atmosphere.

"Yes, my dear, let's enjoy the reception."

Rafique stored his foster mother's warnings to the rear of his mind, opting to do whatever necessary to keep his secret hidden from the world.

The remainder of the wedding reception went without a hitch. Rafique and his closest friends had outdone themselves on the pricey ceremony. The décor was exquisitely selected from a variety of high end party supplier, and the occasion called for everyone to be dressed in white. Rafique had grown tremendously since meeting Fatimah and had adopted different schools of philosophy. He was intrigued by what the color white represented and wanted to bring that purity to his new found marriage.

He and Fatimah stood hand and hand, and greeted the trust as they exited the banquet hall.

"Hey, there you are... you two look so wonderful together!" Norris complimented.

"Thanks, bro," Rafique said to his fraternity brother. "I finally get the chance to meet the mysterious African goddess. I have to admit, after three years of hearing about you but never actually meeting you in person, we all started to believe that maybe Rafique had lost his mind and had an imaginary woman living halfway across the world," Norris laughed.

"Oh no, Norris," Fatimah shared in his laughter. "We have been planning this for quite some time, but with the corrupt government back home, it takes a really long process to actually get the visa, but I'm here now, and to me, it is a dream come true!" Fatimah was excited.

"And your accent is so thick. Wow, you are really the blessed one of us three," Norris engaged in the small talk as Rafique just observed as his best man and best woman comfortably conversed.

"Okay, well nice to finally meet you, Fatimah. I must be heading home. I have to be up bright and early for work in the morning." Norris readied himself to depart and promised to stop by their new home the next day.

The last person to exit was Rafique's foster mother. It was as if the last few days she was sticking around more than often. She had persistently insisted on helping with the wedding and reception, where in the past, she wouldn't even answer his phone calls.

"Okay, Rafique baby," she greeted, I guess I better be going now too, everything seems to be in order here, and I can finally take these heels off!"

Rosaline sashayed off into the parking lot without waiting on a response. Her 5'7, 165 pound frame gracefully headed towards her 2018 Mercedes, leaving her signature White Diamond perfume to continue speaking for her. Her immaculately curled hair graced her shoulders, and her ebony skin tone created no contrast against the night. She wasn't spotted again until the interior light of her vehicle came on, and she eased out of the parking lot.

"She doesn't like me," Fatimah confirmed, not missing that for the second time that Rosaline had not even looked into her direction, let alone offered a greeting.

"Honey, please, pay her no mind." He attempted to comfort his wife. "The truth is, nobody likes her! She is a miserable and scorned woman. She was not invited here tonight! She just barged in because she just has to feel a part of something!" Rafique comforted his wife. "Please don't let her ruin this special night that Allah has created."

"Okay, Rafique baby," Fatimah agreed, choosing to wisely create a good memory of their first night together.

Being raised in poverty and hardship had created awareness and determination in Fatimah, and consciously, she had already concluded that she would keep a close eye on Rosaline. She didn't have any concrete evidence, but she was inclined by her intuition to believe that Rosaline had some animosity towards her.

As the night grew old, Rafique and Rosalind strolled hand and hand down the serene Miami Beach scene. Rafique had promised to show Fatimah his place of serenity. After a brief walk under the exhilarating stars, they finally made it to the secluded ledge overlooking the ocean. The water vehemently assaulted the stone pillars that gracefully supported them. Momentarily, the silence and tranquility engulfed them as the bathed in the afterglow of the moonlight.

"Muslima, this is where I come when I want a piece of mind. Here I just contemplate and marvel at the signs of Allah's greatness. Ironically, this is the same place that I planned to end my life a few years back."

Fatimah just listened. She wasn't the type to pry and would just allow Rafique to confide in her about his suicidal thoughts naturally.

"Rafique, to be honest, those things that you speak of are now irrelevant because those are past circumstances, and I only care about the man that I married now and our future together!"

Fatimah gazed into his eyes casting her strength upon her husband.

"Thanks sweetheart, you have unknowingly supported me through the most vulnerable time of my life."

"Rafique, never praise me, only Allah is worthy of our praises!"

Dusk quickly turned into dawn, and Fatimah and Rafique maneuvered through the deserted suburbs as he navigated his way to his newly purchased town home.

Fatigue sat in as he exited the interstate and turned into the secluded neighborhood where he and his wife would reside and hopefully begin to raise a family.

To be in America was always a fantasy of Fatimah's, so she maintained her alertness as Rafique grew tired.

She was mesmerized by how clean and decorated the streets of Miami Beach were. She looked around at the well-lit shopping malls and marveled at the establishments. As Rafique entered into the housing association, Fatimah couldn't help but to notice a vehicle appearing to be following them.

Not to alert Rafique, she zeroed in and noticed, and watched the car closely.

"Honey, can you give me a tour of the neighborhood?" Fatimah asked, using her intuition to see if her suspicions would be confirmed.

Rafique reluctantly navigated through the gated community doing his best to shake his weariness. He understood Fatimah's anxiety and didn't want to ruin her experience. Little did he know, Fatimah could care less about the tour. She had her attention trained on the dark-colored sedan that mimicked their every move.

"Oh honey, look at this beautiful home!"

She pretended to admire the elegant home to her right. Rafique decreased his speed until the SUV came to a complete stop. Fatimah watched as the trail had no choice but to maneuver around them, and she recorded the license plate number.

"Okay honey, let's go!" she said, anxious to see where the car would turn.

The suspicious sedan made a sharp right, and Fatimah watched as the taillights became engulfed by the darkness of the early morning.

"Fatimah, is everything okay? You seem a bit detached?" Rafique inquired, oblivious to the suspicious activity that Fatimah had just witnessed.

"Yeah, I'm fine, it's just the new surroundings have me dazzled a bit... but I will adapt," she responded, subconsciously vowing to protect her husband at the cost of her own life.

As Rafique and Fatimah pulled into their newly financed town home, Rafique noticed something very odd. The fenced in home was immaculately groomed as usual. The palm trees danced in the moderate wind and cast their unique shadows. Rafique could see the den's light shining through the window, which was normal if you disregard the fact of Rafique's conservative nature. He would never leave an appliance let alone a light on in his house.

"What's wrong?" Fatimah asked, sensing the heightened tension.

"Hold on! Stay in the car!" Rafique demanded. "If you see anything out of the ordinary, just drive off and call 911!"

Rafique cautiously eased toward the house. The door was ajar. He listened for sounds of an intruder but didn't hear the slightest movement. He looked back to see Fatimah staring at him through the windshield. She was still sitting in the passenger's seat. Rafique eased the door open.

"What the fuck?"

What he saw was enough to rob him of his breath. He was speechless, he was confused. Who would break in and ransack his home? Rafique went to lengths to surprise Fatimah by purchasing modest furniture and the latest appliances, and now everything was ruined.

"Oh my!" Fatimah gasped as she crept to his side. "Who?" she began to ask, but when she saw the agony and confusion on her husband's face, she broke down into uncontrollable tears. Rafique couldn't even comfort her because the state of shock consumed him.

The plush loveseats and sectional was sliced multiple times, the stainless-steel end tables were upturned, and the glass tops were shattered. As he examined the entire home, he noticed that every room was in the same condition. Fatimah headed through the house on the heels of her husband.

She pushed the bathroom's door open and gasped loudly. The mirror was shattered and with bold red lipstick was written… UNTIL DEATH DO US!

Rafique continued to ponder about his current demise.

Who, was his first question, followed by why? He searched his most valuable collections and concluded that nothing had been stolen. His intuition and experience led him to believe that someone held a personal vendetta towards him.

Fatimah was already formulating ideas and plans of revenge. Secrets often revealed themselves, but to her, time was an enemy; she needed immediate answers. Circumstances called for desperate measures, and she vowed to protect her investment at all times, even if it meant inviting death.

"Rafique, I don't know what the meaning of all this is, but let's just make a report to the authorities and then lodge at a hotel until we can get to the bottom of this!"

Fatimah sought to comfort her distraught husband. Little did she know, contacting the authorities was the last thing flowing through Rafique's mind. True, Rafique lived the life of a changed man thanks to his Islamic lifestyle, but the former gangster was still hiding within. Rafique was a product of the gruesome city of Over Town, the heart of Miami. Before doing a small stint in the federal penitentiary, that could've easily cost him his life, Rafique was a ruthless assassin. He still held the code of the streets and the Conspiracy of Silence in his heart. Contacting the authorities was a violation of the game!

"Okay, baby," Rafique agreed. "But let me get you out of here first, and I will file a report this afternoon," he lied, breaking one of his vows for a good reason.

They silently drove to a nearby establishment and booked a suite for an entire week. To try and ease the tension of ruining their memory, Rafique reserved the executive suite at the Fontaine Bleau hotel overlooking the beach. The room was above presidential status. It was for a king, and overlooking his shoulder, he could see that his queen was deeply preoccupied with filing her thoughts.

Instead of speaking, Rafique chose to allow his body to communicate for him. He opted to caress her shoulders hoping to remove the building tension. He gently pulled her into his embrace and laid down propping her fragile head on his powerful breast. Exhaustion finally managed to overtake them both, allowing them to be engulfed in a serene slumber. That is until the rays assaulted him through the curtains decorating the seventy-two-inch window.

Rafique reluctantly sat erect, being brought back to the reality of his damaged home and personal possessions. He glanced over and smiled at the blessing that Allah had bestowed upon him. His naturally beautiful life partner was sleeping as if worry could never invade her perfect world.

He quietly showered and prepared for his obligatory prayer. Being a devout Muslim was trying at times, but honoring his oaths to his God and appreciating his favor gave Rafique the motivation that he needed.

Rafique quickly dressed and exited the suite with the keys to his Lincoln Continental in hand. He was on a mission, determined to collect any clues to help him locate the source of his newly inherited trauma. He was adamant about eliminating all potential threats.

Fatimah wisely pretended to not hear Rafique as he prepared for his day. She understood the natural order of life and refused to get in the way of her man's role as protector and provider. Although submissive, Fatimah had the heart of a lioness and would also use her strengths if and when the occasion arose.

As Rafique exited the corridor of the immaculate establishment, he located his sedan and cautiously strolled into its direction. As he entered the vehicle, his cellular sprang to life.

"Hello?" he answered, hoping the unknown caller would reveal a clue to his mystery. Unfortunately, he was met with a dial tone.

As hard as he tried, Rafique couldn't resist the urge to transform into the killer that was naturally within. He had tried to live a pious life, but somebody had just crossed the line by tormenting him and his wife. A line that threatened to drag him past the point of no return. He dialed the number back and was greeted with the automated system that informed him that the number he had dialed was out of service.

His thoughts raced as he ignited his engine and drove to a place he had never expected to see again. He merged into the light traffic on the McArthur Causeway and maneuvered through the vehicles as he aimed for his destination. After about an hour of traveling, he pulled into the cemetery where he had symbolically buried his former life along with his guns and ammunition. He inhaled deeply as he came to his assigned plot and exited the vehicle. The cemetery was deserted and poorly maintained. The ideal location for a life of violence, treachery, and manipulation. He uncovered the tombstone and gained access to its hidden compartment.

Feeling as if someone was watching him, he stopped and surveyed his surroundings. Nothing stood out to him, so he just assumed his anxiety and paranoia was taking its toll. He quickly removed the granite tombstone that was inscribed, "Pressure does one of two things... Bust pipes or make diamonds!"

Seeing the guns that had removed so many men from their families brought chills to his body. He removed the .40 caliber handgun and quickly put them in his small carrier bag. After securing the tombstone back in its place, he swiftly entered his vehicle and eased out of the cemetery in route to his home to assess the damage.

Thoughts consumed him as he drove down I-95, making sure to adjust his cruise control to the speed limit. Rafique pulled into his estate safely, removing his pistol and tucking it on his waist. He examined the property hoping to identify something that was otherwise hidden in the darkness of the early morning. Nothing stood out to him.

He cautiously entered through the rear door of his home, weapon at the ready... he took in the scene... one that reminded him of his past.

He stealthily cleared every room before looking to see if anything of sentimental value was destroyed. He bee lined for his home office that he used for the non-profit organization that he and Fatimah were in the process of founding.

Ironically, the office looked to be the only room untouched. He sought to examine it more closely and eased in the direction of his desktop. His computer was powered on. Curious as to the meaning, he turned on the screen and gasped as he viewed its contents. Again, it read... "UNTIL DEATH DO US PART!"

The images attached were of Fatimah. It showed videos of her getting off of her flight at the Miami international Airport. It showed pictures of the limo that Rafique had sent to transport her to the wedding boutique and then to the mosque. The pictures looked to have been taken from a distance, apparently without Fatimah's knowledge or consent. The final picture was of Fatimah and Rafique walking down the beach hand in hand. Blood animatedly trickled down Fatimah's face.

Rafique urgently dialed Fatimah's phone which was immediately forwarded to the voicemail. Praying that the line was just tied up, he called the phone again. Forwarded!

"Fuck!" he vehemently pondered on the steering wheel hurting his hand in the process. He was almost to the point of hysterics.

Without hesitation, Rafique jetted back to his car, hoping that his wife was safe. As he sat in his sedan, he searched for the number to the hotel, while trying to calm his accelerating heartbeat.

"Hello!" he anxiously answered as the receptionist greeted him.

"Ma'am... this is Rafique Talib. I am occupying the penthouse with my wife, Fatimah Talib! Can you please connect me to the room?" he pleaded.

"Hold for just a second," the young lady responded.

The line seemed to go dead for a few seconds, and then, the receptionist came on the line, "Mr. Talib, the line seems to be busy. Is everything okay?" she sincerely inquired.

"No, I need security to go up and check my suite immediately! My wife may be in danger!" he screamed while racing through the interstate pushing his Lincoln to its limits.

"Okay sir, I will notify security immediately!" she responded. She sensed the urgency in his voice.

Rafique nearly side swiped a large SUV while shifting through the traffic. He didn't know exactly the meaning of the message evident on his computer but was determined to keep Fatimah out of the path of danger. What would he do if his only source of unconditional love was removed from his life? Who would want to hurt her? Was it a result of his former life?

Lost in thought, Rafique almost missed his exit and crossed several lanes just in time to merge into traffic. He arrived at the hotel in record breaking time, oblivious to the risk he had taken driving recklessly with a dirty weapon on his hip.

As he closed in on the hotel, his heart rate accelerated. Before he could see the building, he noticed the emergency lights and continued to hear sirens in the distance. Several squad cars were posted directly in front of the entrance.

He accelerated his speed and came to a halt, double parking his car as close as he could before racing out of the vehicle.

"What's happening?" he demanded to know of the young deputy who was putting up the yellow crime scene tape.

"You cannot...!" the officer started, but refrained from speaking when he noticed the sullen and deranged look in Rafique's eyes. "Are you the husband?" he asked, confirming that something terribly wrong had happened to Fatimah in his absence.

"Tell me she is okay?" he pleaded, with tears in his eyes.

"Sir, when we arrived on the scene, there was no one in the room. There does seem to be sign of struggle on the scene, but we are unclear to as what may have transpired. We are collecting the hotel's video footage, but it seems there was some sort of malfunction with the surveillance this morning. The security personnel says that it's out of the ordinary for the cameras to have failed. We are not exactly sure what we are looking at this morning, and my captain has directed us to handle this as a crime scene," the young deputy briefed Rafique on the latest updates.

Rafique was now passed the point of desperation. He had subjected Fatimah to danger and now didn't even know if she was dead or alive. The lead detective had refused to allow him into the suite. Rafique pondered whether or not to tell the police about the destruction of his home the night before. Just the sight of the officers made Rafique noxious. He knew that no matter what, he would not confide in the same authorities that had attempted to take his life in the past.

Rafique answered a few routines questions for the detective and fled the scene in his Lincoln. He aimlessly drove not knowing where to begin his search. He eventually ended up driving back to his home to dig through the computer for any clue that may lead him to finding Fatimah.

He arrived at his home in a sullen mood. Before entering his office, Rafique took a deep breath to calm his raging nerves. He wanted to be able to observe everything without overlooking vital clues. He turned the desktop back on and began to inspect the computer. He went into the history because someone had to plug in to upload the photos. The history was wiped clean! Out of options, he went back to examine the photos. In one of the pictures, he noticed a partial hand; obviously the hand of the picture taker. He couldn't begin to make out whose hand it was, but he did notice a ring. Unable to clearly make out any distinctive subscriptions, Rafique filed this minute piece of detail in his mind and continued to search the photos. Lost in time and in a mission, Rafique was oblivious to the presence that shared the room with him until he felt the steel of a gun's barrel pressed into the back of his head.

"Do not make a sound," the middle eastern accent directed.

Rafique wisely followed directions and waited for the opportune chance to react.

The unknown perpetrator stood behind Rafique anxious for the opportunity to cash in on his investment. It had been nearly four years since he had concocted the plan to get his revenge on the man that had killed his father and made away with several million dollars.

"Did you think I would just give up my search to find you?" he asked in partial Arabic.

"No, I just didn't think you had the balls, Qasim," Rafique responded, revealing that he knew exactly who held him at gun point.

Qasim hit Rafique with the butt of his pistol causing blood to trickle down the rear of his head.

Rafique knew Qasim as a result of the murders that Rafique committed for Qasim's father who went by the name Bilal. Rafique and Bilal's relationship was prosperous and beneficial for both parties. Bilal was a well-respected and established business man from the east to the west. He imported and exported precious stones in and out of Medina. He always desired to expand his business into America hoping to bring wealth to his country, but because of his religious affiliations, the counter parts placed unrealistic barriers in his path to stone wall his pursuits.

As a result, Bilal sought out his trusted enforcer to eliminate all threats. In the midst of Rafique executing a few of Wall Street's top financiers, Bilal attempted to have Rafique also eliminated, feeling exposed to the assassin.

Being a product of the hood, Rafique always prepared himself for the double cross. He expertly tapped all of Bilal's sources of secure communication after his intuition sensed a foul in the game. After collecting evidence of an ambush, Rafique reversed the roles and changed the game for his present and his future. Rafique set out to accomplish his hired task but doubled back and eliminated Bilal after torturing him until access to his hidden treasures were in Rafique's hands.

Rafique vowed to never expose his weaknesses. He just sat there as Qasim began to speak. "The entire time my father had you working for him, he looked down on me because I was weak!" Qasim began to cry which scared Rafique more than anything. An unstable man with a gun was the worst signs of ultimate destruction. "He ignored me because of you... He denied me the right to be called his son! All I ever wanted was to show him just how strong I was, and now I get the chance to show him! Turn around and look at me, you bastard! I want to look you in the eyes before I close them for good!"

Rafique slowly turned and was flabbergasted at what he saw. Fatimah stood there pointing the pistol at the back of his head. When she spoke, her voice was that of Qasim's, but she had the beauty of a goddess.

"What the fuck!" he subconsciously screamed.

"Yeah, that's right," Qasim continued to speak." I have been working on this plan for about four long years. I didn't contact you by mistake. I just knew that with your experience and stature, I had to come correct. All the emails and the late phone calls... All the letters... they were all a part of this cake I had baking for you. The easiest access to a wounded man is his heart, so I went through several operations to gain this feminine appearance and it worked out great because you never got to touch me and notice that I never had surgery to remove my penis."

Rafique stared into what he knew as Fatimah's eyes calculating his next move.

"You took something from me, and I'm sure that you cannot bring it back! You stole my dignity! You robbed me of my relationship with my father, and you stole what I was supposed to inherit, and I want what was mine... and I want yours!"

Rafique was at a loss for words. Instinctively, he sought a possible escape from his potentially dangerous situation.

Qasim had staged the entire scene at the hotel only to distract Rafique long enough to put his plan into motion. Rafique calculated what it would take to safely remove the weapon from Qasim who stood firm with both hands glued to the Smith and Wesson revolver. Qasim was clearly emotional, and from Rafique's experience, he knew that Qasim was the worst type of murderer under those conditions. Rafique was unsure as to how he would remove the gun without being harmed in the process. Being a self-taught psychological genius, he opted to calm Qasim's raging nerves and manipulate him into a safer position.

"Qasim, I am terribly sorry for your loss physically, and even more, emotionally. Being the strong-minded man that you've obviously become, I know you will understand my position. I was loyal to your father. I have risked my life more times than I can count to make sure that his endeavors were all prosperous. His back was against the wall, and he attempted to commit the ultimate betrayal!"

Rafique wouldn't whimper even if death stared him in the face. Rafique had danced with death all of his life. As an adolescent, he had watched as his biological mom was raped and brutally murdered. Wounded and traumatized, he was placed in the Department of Children and Families foster care program. After several years of being relocated from center to center, Rafique was finally fostered by Rosalina. She never really cared for anyone's wellbeing but her own.

The funds that she received from the state's funding program never went to the care of the children in her custody. Instead, Rosalinda funded her glamorous life by spoiling herself with diamonds, furs, and expensive clothing.

Rafique was always expected to act as her personal slave. At times, Rosalina would get drunk and lash out on Rafique for no reasonable reason. Rafique never understood how a human could treat another the way that his foster mother had treated him.

Looking for a means to escape the physical and mental agony, Rafique turned to the life of the streets. He sought love and ultimately allowed the pimps, whores, drug dealers, and murderers to raise him. At the age of sixteen, Rafique's hand was forced when one of Rosalina's many boyfriends had attempted to molest him. Rafique was left no choice but to kill him in cold blood and was ultimately acquitted of all charges because of the overwhelming evidence of the pedophile's previous record of abuse.

The first of many murders, Rafique felt the radiating power of what taking another's life felt like. He had never felt so large in his life and bathed in the glory of having what he felt was the ultimate strength. Now as he stared down the barrel of Qasim's gun, he flashed back into the events that led him to this particular situation. Qasim was to the point of tears, and Rafique could see how unsure of himself and unstable he had become.

"Qasim, I hope you understand that in this world, it's the survival of the fittest, and Bilal was going to have me executed, so I had to preserve my life, but if you must remove me from this world, then I will embrace death."

Rafique closed his eyes as he envisioned the paradise that Allah had prepared for him. He was comfortable with himself and his accomplishments as a man.

He could smell the success that Allah and his messengers would welcome him with. He braced himself and waited until he heard the loud blast from the revolver.

Rafique didn't know how death would feel, but he waited to see what would transpire next until he felt a trembling hand on his shoulder. He opened his eyes to see Rosalina standing next to him with a small compact weapon in her hand. He glanced over top see Qasim faced down lying in a pool of his own blood.

"Rafique, I know I let you down as a child, but since then, I have always waited for the chance to show you how much I have really loved you as my son. I can never take back the terrible past that I helped create for you, but I can and will play my part to show you how sorry I am if you let me. After the wedding when you left, I couldn't help but admire your accomplishments in life. As I watched you, I noticed a vehicle trail you, and I had to see to it that you were safe. Rafique, I have always wanted a son like you, and when I was gifted with you, I couldn't appreciate the gift, but I do love you, son, and I will forever Until Death Do Us!"

Soulja Choc Presents Authors

For The Love of Money

By
Mo-Nique

Chapter One

    I envisioned myself in a movie I'll forever consider a classic. It's called the Players Club, and there was one line in particular that stands out to me and my life. "Make that money, don't let it make you." Now, when Diana Armstrong/Diamond told those new strippers that in the movie, I didn't understand what she meant by it, but now, my level of understanding has increased drastically.

    Ronnie was my favorite character. See, through the eyes of a child, she had it all; she had money, a nice car, clout, niggas chasing her, and I wanted to be just like her. I began using Ronnie as a guide making sure I asked myself what Ronnie would do in every situation, but unfortunately for me, my life took a drastic turn. I soon learned that everything that glitters isn't gold.

Marisa Murray (Truth be told)

From the age of fourteen, I never lived a normal life. Up until that point, I had been raised by my aunt and uncle who were the best parents in the world to me. They had three kids of their own, but when I was three and left home on my own, they made the decision to care for me as one of their own.

Even as a young child, I knew something wasn't right about my mom. She just wasn't like anyone else I had ever seen. She didn't dress up like my Grandma Pat, she didn't comb her hair or mine either for that fact like I saw my aunties do my cousins, and if it wasn't for being constantly left at other people's houses, I wouldn't know what a kitchen was for because we never had a need to go in ours. I also believed that we had a big family because every man that came over was my uncle, and there was a lot of them.

I didn't know any better until one day when I was around twelve, I was curious and asked my Aunt Janet where all my uncles were and why they never came around to visit me after I showed them love. She asked me what I meant by that, and I told her how I gave them kisses on their lips and on their private places and hugs afterwards when they gave me treats and money. I told her how my mom, would say I was a good daughter, pat me on the back, and take my money to put it up, but let me keep the snacks. My Aunt Janet immediately started crying and shaking her head no, and that was the first time in years I felt like it was something wrong with what I did.

I started crying too, but I didn't know why. My auntie sat me down at the kitchen table and explained to me what had happened to me and that my mom, Risha, used me to fund her drug habit and that I only had two uncles, Chris and Michael, who I saw regularly. My life changed that day as far as how I viewed people, especially men and my trifling mom. My aunt and uncle put me in counseling, and I did my best to still live as a happy kid, until my fourteenth birthday when my mom showed up with the cops and snatched me away from the good life I become so accustomed to.

Six months later (Back with Risha)

I was angry as fuck when I was forced to leave the best home I had ever known. Risha had never been a good mother. In the past few years she, hadn't been one at all. The nerve of her to show up on my auntie's door steps with the police demanding her child. Shit, up until that moment, I didn't think she even remembered she had a child she was gone for so long.

Supposedly, she was getting herself together. The first three months was nice; I lived somewhat like a teenager. Risha was working at the post office and had moved into a nice three-bedroom apartment in Conyers, Georgia, a very upscale neighborhood. She drove a little Honda Accord that was only a couple years old, she kept the house stocked with food and made home cooked meals and was even keeping our hair and nails done weekly. She even had a steady boyfriend. I really was proud of the fact that Risha was trying to be a mom, but you know what they say, all good things come to an end.

On the fourth month, I came home on a Tuesday afternoon, and Risha was still home along with her boyfriend, Tell a.k.a Montell and another young man that looked to about twenty. I guess I interrupted their conversation because when I walked in, everyone got quiet and was staring at me.

"Hey," I spoke to no one in particular

They all replied, "Hi," back simultaneously. I walked past the living room and went in the kitchen to get something to drink before going to my room. Risha stopped me coming out the kitchen and told me to come here; she wanted me to meet someone. Ugh...this is exactly what I didn't want. I already thought the young-looking stranger was cute, but I didn't want to meet nobody looking like this. The curls had fallen out my hair, and I was sweaty from running for the bus, but I did as I was told. With my juice in my hand, I walked into the living room.

"Marisa, this is Antonio, Tell's little brother; he is going to be staying with us for a while," Risha said, pulling on a cigarette.

He stood up and extended his hand for me to shake, but I was still staring at Risha with a mug on my face.

"And why would he be staying with us when he has a whole brother sitting right there with a house of his own?" I questioned because that just didn't make sense to me.

"Because this my damn house, and you don't pay no bills here and I need money," Risha snapped.

I was so mad I could have slapped Risha's ass. I was just getting to the point of trying to form some type of relationship with her, now she wanted to bring some stranger in to live with us.

Lanes of Love

When I saw Montell and his brother laughing and shaking their heads, I didn't say another word. I just turned around and walked to my room. I needed someone to talk to, so I pulled out my phone and called my best friend, Me'chelle.

She finally answered just as I was about to hang up. "Hey, best friend," she said.

"It took you long enough, what the hell was you doin'?"

Chapter Two

Me'Chelle

As soon as I picked up the phone, I could tell by the tone in my best friend's voice that something wasn't right, and whatever it was pissed her off. After about five minutes into the conversation, she explained to me that her mom just pulled a fast one on her by dropping the bomb that she was moving her boyfriend's little brother in with them. Marisa wasn't happy about it, not one bit.

"Me'Chelle!" my drunk as always father called my name. "Come here now!" He continued.

"Girl, let me go. My dad's drunk ass is calling for me," I said to Marisa.

"Ok. Call me later," she replied.

Raising up from the edge of my bed, I did as he demanded and walked towards the family room where he was. I walked down the five flights of stairs and stood in front of the couch.

"Yes dad, you called me?" I said.

He leaned up and handed me his glass demanding that I bring him some ice so he could fix him another drink. He was already two glasses in on his normal drink, bumpy face, dry Gin with a splash of 7Up. I knew if I said anything it would cause an argument, which on a regular basis would lead into a physical altercation. I wasn't in the mood to go there with him today, so I took the glass and walked towards the kitchen to get the ice.

I walked back to the family room and handed him the glass of ice and tried to escape before he asked for something next, but it was too late.

"Me'chelle, who the fuck were you on the phone with? I know you not on my phone that I pay the bill for without my permission," he said to me with that tone that he wanted to pick a fight.

"Here you go," I said.

"What you say to me?" he said as he raised up from the couch to slap me across my face. I stopped his arm which lead to him snatching me up by the collar of my shirt. As he got in my face to yell, I could smell the liquor and cigarettes on his breath. With his grip around my collar, he threw me with all his drunken might across the room. My back hit the corner of the wall, and I let out a huge whelp. Without any concern of what he just did, he walked over to me and told me to get up and get out of his face.

I tried to get up, but the pain that shot up my back caused me to let out another whelp. This time, it irritated him more, and he raised his size ten shoe and kicked me back towards the wall.

"Dad no, please stop," I pleaded.

"You're so weak, just like your momma," he responded. "Now get the fuck up and out my fuckin' face before I give you some more."

This time, I got up quickly and ignored the pain that was shooting up my back and now into my rib cage. I ran into my room, laid down on my bed with my face into the pillow, and cried. Crying into the pillow was something I learned at an early age, so he wouldn't hear me. The more he heard me cry, the more agitated he would get. I tried to stay out of his way in order to avoid the fights. It seemed as though the older I got, the more he found ways to pick a fight with me. I had two other sisters, but he only attacked me. I made sure of it. I would kill him if I ever heard or saw him go after my little sisters the way he attacked me.

I woke up at three a.m. I guess I cried myself straight to sleep. In three more hours, I would be getting up to get ready for school. Checking on my little sisters in the other room first, I walked into the bathroom to run a hot bath. I knew my dad was passed out and wouldn't hear me up and about, so I took my time. I poured some Epsom salt into the tub along with some bubble bath so I could sooth the pain in my back and on my rib cage. The pain was worse now than it was before. I just knew there had to be a huge bruise on my back. I walked over to the mirror that hung behind the door to check my sides. As suspected, I had a huge black and purple bruise on my right side where he kicked me. I wanted to cry as I stood there looking at the damage done to my body from my very own father.

The water wasn't too hot, so I slowly lowered myself into the tub. I soaked for about an hour and then washed up and got out. Before leaving the bathroom, I made sure the tub was cleaned. Lord forbid that I leave a dirty tub for him to find. I walked into my room with the towel wrapped around my body. I walked over to my dresser and grabbed the Palmer's Cocoa Butter and deodorant. Not getting dressed, I put on an oversized t-shirt and laid back down in bed until it was time for me to get up for school. I couldn't wait to see Marisa. I needed my friend right about now.

Chapter Three

Marisa

    I woke up again this morning to an empty house and an empty refrigerator. This shit had become second nature around here ever since Montell called it quits with my mom Risha, more Risha than my mom; she had yet to earn that title mainly because of shit like this.

    I didn't know why I was so surprised because if I hadn't been stealing or getting money from Antonio every now and then, I would have starved to death. I'm not going to lie, I really had high hopes for my mom this time. For a while, she was doing everything right, then two months ago, everything changed. I came home from school, and Risha was laid out on the sofa with her hair sprawled all over her head. She had a two-piece camisole set and a terry cloth bathrobe on, cradling a bottle of 1800 when she should have been at work.

Her appearance struck me as odd, so I dropped my book bag in the foyer and went over to make sure she was okay. I stood in front of the sofa calling her name before I started to gently shake her. She barely opened her eyes to look at me. Before, she grumbled and tried to turn over, but I wouldn't let her. I took the bottle from her hand and made her sit up on the sofa.

"Ma! Ma! What's wrong?" I asked.

When she lifted her head up to look at me, it was the first time I saw true hurt in her eyes. She threw her arms around my neck and cried into my shoulder. "Marisa, he left me and went back to his wife and kids," she sobbed uncontrollably.

"Sshh...it's okay..." I tried to assure her, but in the back of my mind, I knew something wasn't right with him. I did the best I could to comfort her. I even made her some hot tea to try and sober her up. I had never seen her like that before; her hands were shaking as she told me word for word about how he stopped by and told her he needed to talk to her. She went onto explain that she cooked him a nice lunch because he was just coming off the road from a two-week job, and she wanted it to be special.

The whole time she was talking, I couldn't help but to think, Damn, she has never gone all out for me like that, her own child, but I continued to listen anyway waiting on the other shoe to fall.

"So after we ate and went to sit down in the living room, he got on his knees in front of me, Marisa. I thought for sure he was going to ask me to marry him after all we had been through, but instead, he told me that he was married with a set of twins, and that he was ready to put his family back together and be the man he should have been all along,"

Risha said, taking the bottle of alcohol out my hand and turning it up straight.

That was the first day of many to come of her sinking deeper and deeper into alcohol and drugs, and I wasn't the only one that noticed either. Antonio had started trying to spend more time with me and bringing me food home because once again, Risha had the house looking like she was allergic to cleaning it or going to a grocery store. The more time I spent with him, I learned a lot about him including the fact that his brother's wife had accused him of trying to sleep with her, and Montell didn't trust him being there, so he offered to find him somewhere else to go, and since my mom was his side chick, what better place for him then here?

Antonio and I had started fooling around shortly after he moved in. He used to help me with my homework, take me to visit my friends, we even went to the movies and out to eat, and I was falling hard for him. Even with the six-year age difference, he never treated me like a child and wasn't ashamed to be seen with me and my friends around town. He was the first dude to ever show me love, and I didn't want to lose that, so I took care of his needs, and he took care of mine. He would give me money for clothes, to get my nails and hair done, or to just hang out with Me'chelle, but lately, even he was leaving me to fend for myself. He had not been home in days and barely answered my phone calls, and on the rare occasion that he did pick up, he would feed me some bullshit about how he had business to handle.

I knew what Antonio did in the streets, and that hustling had no set hours, but over the last few months, he was the most stable thing I had going for myself outside of Me'chelle, and now, his actions were becoming suspect. Not wanting to believe what my mind was telling me, I just went ahead and took a shower, so I could get ready for school.

Ten minutes later, I was stepping out the shower. I dried off and wrapped the towel around my body and went in my room closing the door. Even though I was alone, I guess some things were just force of habit. Reaching on my dresser for my Victoria Secret "Rush" lotion to apply to my dark skin, I slipped on a pair of boy shorts and a matching sports bra, compliments of my mother before she fell off the bandwagon, then walked over to my closet to pull out my floral Adidas suit and a pink v-neck t-shirt to go underneath, and my new black Adidas with the floral stripes. I gelled my shoulder length hair in a ponytail, sprayed on my Rush body spray, grabbed my book bag, and headed to the bus stop. I looked forward to going to school every day just so I could see my bestie, Me'chelle. As soon as the bus pulled up in front of the school, I saw her pacing back and forth like something was wrong. I instantly felt my body heat rise because I didn't play about my friend; whoever had done something to her was going to feel these hands.

Move!" I shouted, pushing some boy with a band case out the way. My friend was upset, so this was an emergency. As soon as she saw me, her eyes lit up like she was glad to see me, and everything was alright. I understood because she had that same effect on me. It was like nobody else could relate to our situation but us. I reached out to give her a hug like I did every morning, and she squealed out in pain scaring me. I didn't know what happened, but somebody was finna pay for putting their hands on someone I loved like a sister.

Chapter Four

Me'chelle

It'd been months and the beatings were getting worse. I was no longer able to hide the bruises nor the pain. This morning as I was getting dressed for school, I stared at myself in the mirror for what seemed like five minutes, but really about thirty seconds. Staring at the fresh knot on my right temple and the bruise on my side, I didn't know how much longer I could take this. Every day I thought about packing up in the middle of the night and disappearing, but who would look after my sisters? The twins, Sherrelle and Nicole were turning ten in a few days.

Lanes of Love

I'd been the only mother figure in their life for a while, and if I left now, I would never forgive myself if he went after them next.

Fighting through the pain in each step I took, I walked slowly to the bus stop. I couldn't wait to see my best friend and tell her the master plan I was up all night coming up with. We both needed to get out these hell holes we called home. If I knew her as I thought I did, there was no way she was turning down this opportunity.

"Hey, best friend," I said as she reached out to hug me. "Ouch," I continued.

The look she gave me was a look of death. I didn't have to say what happened, she already knew.

"It takes every bit of good that's left in me not to run up in the middle of the night and take care of your problem, Me'chelle. I hate that you're going through this. I really do. Why do you stay around?" Marisa asked.

"If I leave, he'll take it out on the twins, and I will definitely kill him then. Then with him gone, and me being locked up, who's going to look after them then?" I responded.

"I get it. I get it. It's just kills me to see you in so much pain. We have to do something about it," she replied

This was the opening I needed to bring up my solution.

"Well, since you brought it up. I was up all night coming up with a master plan for the both of us. We can make some real good money and get out of this hell we call life right now. After school, let's walk home, and I can discuss it more with you. I don't want any ear hustlers listening in."

She gave me the ok as the bus pulled up. We walked to our regular seats and sat down.

***

The two o'clock bell rang, indicating that school was over. I walked out of my history class and met Marisa in the hallway by the lockers. She looked sad, which wasn't like her. At this time of the day, she was excited to be leaving school.

"What's wrong? What happened?" I asked her. She went to explaining to me how Antonio hadn't been home, and she couldn't reach him. Marisa wasn't the type to worry over anyone, but the non-response was bothering her.

"I have so many crazy thoughts going through my head. I don't know what to think, Chelle," she said.

"He'll show up. Quit worrying. He's just being a man," I told her.

"Yeah, you're right. Now to this master plan you have. What's up, girl?" she asked

"Let's talk at the park behind the school," I answered.

It took us ten minutes to walk around the school and to the park. We found a bench by the recreation center to sit. I pulled out my note book my mom left me where I wrote everything down.

"Ok. I have to make it quick since Mr. will be looking for me soon, so this is what I was thinking. You know how I told you my dad's friend approached me to go on a date with him the other day?"

"Yeah."

"What if we start accepting the offers from these older men to take us out? We'll create this fantasy that we'll be their toys in exchange

Lanes of Love

for money? They take us out on dates and etcetera, but they have to pay. They'll be our "sponsors."

"Girl. That's playing with fire. This is your master plan?"

"Think about it. We'll get in good with them, and when they start getting too involved, we'll disappear and leave them hanging dry. It can work, trust. The first one will be my dad's friend Mr. Robert. After I'm done with him, I'll introduce you, and you'll get on with him. There's no way he'll refuse. He's real thirsty," I explained.

"I don't know, Chelle. This seems dangerous. You don't think we're too young?"

"The life we live, we're damn near grown. It's time for us to start making money. I'm tired of living in that house. I need to take my sisters and run away somewhere, but I need money and quickly."

"I hear you. Let me think on it, and I'll have your answer tomorrow morning when I see you at the bus stop. Now, get goin' before your dad starts trippin'."

"Ok. Don't play. I'm going on with the plan if you're in or not. I need this, Risa."

We both got up from the bench and started walking down the street towards our neighborhood. The walk felt like forever today. Maybe because of the anticipation of what Marisa was thinking and would say tomorrow. I just knew she would be onboard. Her reply threw me for a loop.

We reached her house first and said our goodbye's.

"I'll see you in the morning," Marisa said.

"Ok," I replied.

It took me another five minutes to get home. As soon as I opened the door, the smell of alcohol hit my nose. I knew what type of night I was headed towards.

"ME'CHELLE," my drunken dad said from the family room. "What took you so damn long? Your sisters will be here any minute, and who's going to walk them from the bus stop? I know you don't think I was. You need your ass whooped."

"Dad, I'll get the girls," I replied.

"I know that. When you come back, we're gonna talk."

Lanes of Love

Chapter Five

Antonio

    I had Angela bent over the island in the kitchen beating her pussy up. This was our third round, and I was showing out in that pussy using all my moves. I slowed down because being the freak I am, I wanted to watch my dick slide in and out of her creamy walls while she screamed my name. I loved watching her ass shake when she threw it back on me.

    "Damn baby," I moaned watching her do her magic on my dick. Her pussy fit like a condom on my dick. I felt her legs buckling, so I picked her up and carried her to the couch in the living room.

Her body was glistening with sweat as I sat down positioning her on my lap so she could ride me. She leaned in and gave me a passionate kiss, and I could still smell and taste the peach flavored wine she was drinking before we started. The way she gently sucked my tongue into her mouth had me rock hard. She started kissing me on my neck and slowly rocking on my dick. I popped her soft big ass.

"Ride this dick like daddy like it and quit playin'," I demanded making her speed up the pace. "Hell yeah, that's it, baby. Ride daddy dick." I grabbed her by the waist so I could go deeper inside of her

She moaned and begged me to fuck her harder. I flipped her over on her back and lifted her leg over my shoulder and stroked her harder until I felt her walls tighten up and grip my dick.

"Baby, baby," she panted. "I'm about to cum!" she yelled before her body began to shake and tremble. Her pussy gripped my dick so hard I couldn't pull out before I nutted all in her, I immediately regretted not using protection with her. I jumped up and grabbed my phone off the coffee table because it had been ringing constantly while we were fucking, and went into the bathroom, leaving her on the couch looking confused.

I closed the bathroom door and leaned my head and arm against it. "Fuck! I can't believe I let that shit happen," I mouthed.

Just as my phone started ringing again in my hand, I looked down at it and saw it was Marisa calling again. I thought about answering it, but changed my mind when I heard Angela knocking on the bathroom door. "Antonio, is everything alright, did I do something wrong?" she questioned.

"Nawl, everything is fine. I'm just about to take a quick shower; I have to make a run soon," I lied through my teeth cutting the shower on for dramatic effects. I sat on the toilet and went through my missed calls. I saw I had two missed calls from my brother, one from my homie Drake, and four from Marisa. I needed to take a shower before I returned anybody's calls; that always helped me think more clearly. The bathroom was filling up with steam, so I quickly undressed and got in.

I let the hot water run down my body while I lathered my rag with my Suave for men's body wash. I tried to get my mind on making this money, but flashes of Marisa kept invading my thoughts. I hadn't been home in almost a week, and I was starting to miss the time we spent together laughing, watching movies, and just talking until we fell asleep.

The last time we made love, I realized I was falling hard for her. I knew I had to pull away because Angela was becoming suspicious and wondered why I never had time for her anymore. If she didn't know where I stayed, I would have stayed away from her long ago. I finished taking my shower and dried off. I lotioned my body and wrapped a towel around my waist before I walked out the bathroom and into the bedroom, so I could get dressed. When I walked in, Angela was laying across the bed watching a Lifetime movie.

I walked to the closet to get an outfit out. I pulled out a pair of dark blue True Religion jeans with a white and navy blue True Religion shirt, then I walked to my drawer in her dresser to get my Nautica boxers and wife beater. When I turned around, Angela was sitting up staring at me with her arms folded. "So, that's it, we fuck and then you up and leave?" she barked

"Look Angela, don't start that. I have money to make, and I can't get it laying up all day," I told her.

While I was getting dressed, my phone started ringing. I was praying it wasn't a female because I saw Angela trying to lean up and see my screen on the sly. When I saw it was my brother Tell calling, I let out a breath I didn't even know I was holding.

"Yeah?" I answered. I listened to where he wanted to meet and told him I would be there in twenty and hung up. I walked to the nightstand and put on my Cuban link necklace with the Jesus piece, sprayed my Curve cologne, picked up my keys and wallet and went to head for the door. I stopped at the edge of the bed and asked Angela was she going to walk me out. She stopped pouting and started smiling crawling off the bed. I gave her a pop on the ass. "You better stop all that acting crazy; you know daddy got money to make," I told her as we walked to front door together.

    I kissed her briefly on the lips and ran down the steps to my car. I hopped in my '16 Chevrolet Cruze. I didn't even let it warm up, I was just glad to be out the house. I felt like I was being held hostage by Angela. I linked my phone to my car Bluetooth and pulled off to meet my brother at the spot. The radio was jamming. SZA's "The weekend" came on, and my mind flashed back to Marisa. I felt like shit the way I was doing her. She was a good girl; she had been through a lot already, and if I was to be honest with myself, she had my heart, but I felt like I owed Angela for holding a nigga down when I was down the road and she was still spoiling me. If she found out about Marisa, after she beat both of our ass, she would be gone for sure, and if Marisa found out about Angela, I would be one more person to break her heart. What am I going to do? Damn, man.

Chapter Six

Marisa

    I walked in the house and saw my mom sitting at the table shaking her leg and smoking a cigarette zoned out like she wasn't even here. I could tell she was high on something. I wanted to be mad at her for allowing herself to get back on drugs because of a no-good ass man, but instead, I felt sorry for her. I went over to hug her and say hi, and she jumped like I scared her when I was sure she heard me come in the door.

    "Hey, ma," I spoke.

    She looked at me with her glossy eyes like it was her first time seeing me. "Hey, baby." She stood up to hug me but almost fell.

"I bought you a sandwich to eat in the fridge," she said sitting back down in the chair.

"Thank you, ma, but did you eat something?" I asked looking at how small she was getting.

"Yeah, sweetie, mama ate earlier," she replied, but I knew she was lying.

I walked in the kitchen to get the sandwich she bought me. I thought maybe it was from Subway or Kroger, but when I opened the fridge, it was a small sandwich on wheat bread in a plastic ziploc bag and two small cartons of orange juice like they served at school. I took the sandwich and one of the cartons of juice and went to my room. This shit is depressing, I thought, going in my room and closing the door.

I turned on the TV to watch Jerry Springer; he always made me laugh with his sly ass comments and funny antics. I sat on the bed putting my juice on top of my history book and opened my sandwich to eat it. I was so hungry, I only took three bites, and it was gone. I washed it down with the carton of orange juice. I was still hungry, but with no money, that was going to have to do. If I didn't find a job or rich man, I was going to start looking like my mama soon.

I wanted to call Antonio, but what was the use? He wasn't going to answer. I decided to call my Aunt Janet. I hadn't been keeping in contact since they moved away to South Carolina for my uncle's job.

I picked up the phone and dialed her number. It rung three times before she answered, "Hey, Auntie's baby!" she screamed with excitement. "How are you doing? How is school? Why are you just calling me?" she bombarded me with questions before I could answer any. When she ran out of breath and questions, I told her school was good. I told her I was running track and making good grades. We made small talk for a while, enjoying catching up, and she was telling me all of my cousin's business, and we laughed, then she asked the question that I was hoping to avoid, "And how is your mom doing, baby girl?"

"She okay, auntie," I replied with no type of emotion.

"Marisa, you never were a good liar; what's really going on? You know you can tell me anything," she questioned.

I took a deep breath and told my auntie the truth. I told her how good Risha was doing at first when she was working, keeping our hair and nails done regularly, spending time with me and had a steady boyfriend. I told her how I came home from school one day, and she was drunk and passed out and that that was probably the day she relapsed, soon after that, she lost her job, and things had been going downhill ever since.

"Marisa, why didn't you call me or your grandma? How are y'all eating and paying bills?" she asked.

"I don't know Auntie, we barely have food, but nothing has been cut off yet, so I guess at least she's paying bills." I confessed.

"Are you by a grocery store?" she asked.

"Yes, there is a Kroger on the next block," I said.

"Look, I don't have a lot, but walk up there now. I am going to Western Union you some money for food and necessities," my auntie said. "You know you don't have to live like that; you will always have a place with us," she spat. I could tell she was upset.

"I know, but she needs me. Without me, she has nobody but her junkie friends," I admitted.

"Okay baby, I won't pressure you, but my offer always stands, and if you're determined to stay there, at least try to get her in rehab," she said before our goodbyes.

When I got off the phone, I had mixed emotions. I felt like I had betrayed my mom by telling her secret that she obviously didn't want anyone knowing, or I'm sure she would have reached out to my grandma if she did, but at the same time, I felt relieved that I could at least have a decent meal tonight.

I went in my closet and got a jacket out so I could walk to the store. When I passed by the living room, I didn't see my mom at the table, but I heard a noise in the hallway bathroom, so I knew she was home. I started to knock but decided against because I didn't want to know what she was doing, so I walked on past and out the front door.

The walk to the store was nice. I saw all kinds of things that made me smile: kids playing and laughing, nice cars and houses, couples hugged up, and I realized I wanted to live like this. There was more to life than just going to school and coming home to an empty house or to a mom that lived and looked like she was about to die any minute now.

I could see it now, me, Me'chelle, and her sisters in our own place, away from all our problems. I wanted to get my best friend away from her abusive ass dad. I wished he would die already. I was so wrapped up in my thoughts that I bumped right into this fine ass brown skinned boy with thick, long cornrows in his head.

"Oops, I'm sorry," I said as he grabbed me to keep me from falling.

"You okay, Miss lady? What's your name?"

I got myself together and spoke, "Yes, I'm fine. My name is Marisa," I replied.

"Yes, you are fine. I'm KJ," he said looking at me slyly. "Where are you so in a rush to go?" he asked being nosey.

I blushed. "On the next block to the store," I replied.

"Hop in. I will take you," he offered.

"Naw, I'm fine. I will walk; I need the exercise," I politely said and continued my walk.

"I hope I see you again!" he yelled at my back.

The more I walked, the more I thought about what Me'chelle said. Maybe it wouldn't be so bad because if I was ever going to leave this place behind, we needed money. I thought about all the money we could make. Yeah, I was going to tell her I was down with her plan tomorrow.

Chapter Seven

Me'chelle

Six Months Later.......

It'd been six months since Marisa agreed to go with my "Sponsor" plan, and a lot had occurred since that day. For one, we graduated from high school. I didn't think it was going to be possible due to all the missed days of school we had, but we made it. As I lay in my bed after waking up to my alarm clock going off, indicating that my time to get ready for my next date was here, I started to reminisce back on graduation day.

"Me'Chelle Gilmore," I heard the principal say as he stood in front of the stage waiting on me to shake his hand and grab my diploma. I walked across with my head high, shoulders back, and had a huge smile on my face. I grabbed my diploma and shook hands with the staff. Glancing into the crowd, I noticed I didn't see any of my family. Not being surprised, I continued to walk back to my seat. Why would they show up? They hadn't supported or been around in years? Today shouldn't be any different. I brushed the feeling off. I refused to allow anything to mess my day up.

A week after graduation, I celebrated my eighteenth birthday. Marisa and I reserved a hotel room and had girl's night. That was all I wanted, to hang out with my girl and pig out all night. We brought all different sorts of snacks. Like pizza, chips, soda, chocolate, popcorn, and etc. We laughed, watched TV, and planned out our first Sponsor date. The next morning, as we were checking out of the hotel room, I took a deep breath; knowing that I would be able to leave the house of hell, as I called it and be able to provide for the twins was a relief. All I needed to do now was get things going so I could save money.

I got out of bed and walked over to the closet to pull out my outfit for tonight's date. Tonight was being spent with Sponsor Three, as I nicknamed him. We met at the grocery store last week as I was picking up some things to make dinner for the girls. He walked over to the line where I was standing, waiting on my turn to check out.

"Excuse me, miss, I can't help but notice how beautiful you are. What's your name, lovely?" he asked.

"Me'Chelle," I responded.

"Would it be too much to ask for your number?"

I took a quick glance at his gold Rolex watch and Gucci slippers, and thought to myself, He must have money. No one in their right mind would come outside in their Gucci slippers let alone go to the grocery store in them.

I grabbed my phone from out of my purse, and he handed me his. I called my phone from his phone so I would be able to lock my number in his contacts. Ever since that day, he had called nonstop. At first, it was only to so say, "Hello," he says. After about the fifth call, he started to ask if I would let him take me out. I agreed, and here we are today.

I pulled out my favorite short, black, fitted dress that hugged every curve of my size seven frame just right. Looking to see what shoes would match, I settled on my Nine West open toe heels where the strap wrapped around my ankle to buckle. Sponsor Three, as I named him, wasn't as old as Sponsor One or Sponsor Two. He was actually very attractive. Forty-years-old, chocolate skin tone, muscular body with hazel eyes.

Ring...ring...ring... I ran over to my night stand where I had my phone on the charger.

"Hello," I answered.

"What you got goin', fast ass?" Marisa asked.

"Getting ready for my date with Three."

"Oh, yeah, I forgot. Well, have a good time. Do I need to stand by my phone just in case you need an escape?" she asked

"I'll text you if I need you."

"Ok. I'll let you get back to your night. Love you, girl. Remember, make the money..." and before she could finish, I responded, "But don't let the money make you."

"That's right, girl. Do you know where he's taking you?"

"He said something about going dancing. I just hope it ain't at a club. I absolutely hate the club scene. Having drunk people waste their drink on you all night after you took hours getting ready to meet someone is not the sound of fun to me."

"You don't like them because you're not able to get into nothing but the eighteen and up clubs. Yeah, at those clubs, things can get out of control and rowdy. Wait until you're twenty-one or can get a fake ID. We getting' a party bus and club hoppin' all night," Marisa stated.

"What you said, but let me finish getting ready girl, and I'll text you when he picks me up," I said.

Sponsor Three's only request was to see my legs if I was to wear a dress. I thought at first it was weird, but then again, who cared? As long as he continued to open up his wallet, he could see all the legs and ankles he wanted. I placed the dress on my bed and went into the bathroom to take my shower. As I started the water, I overheard my drunken dad walk into his room and close the door. It was only a matter of time before he passed out and wouldn't wake up until tomorrow. I took that opportunity to handle my business. When he woke up, he couldn't even tell I was out all night.

Ring….ring…. ring.. "Hello," I answered again aggressively.

"Whoa, sweetie. You woke up on the other side of the bed today or something? I don't want to bother you, I was just wondering when you needed me to start meeting you at the 7-Eleven?" Three asked.

I had all my sponsors meet me at the 7-Eleven around the corner from the house. All those except my drunken dad's friend at least. He was the only one who knew where I lived, but if it was up to me, he wouldn't know either. I wanted to keep my personal life just that, personal.

"Well, hello, sir. Give me about an hour or so, and I'll be ready," I responded.

"Ok sweetie, I can't wait to see your beautiful face again."

***

Seven o'clock came faster than expected. I heard my phone going off, but I wasn't in the mood to answer a series of questions as to why I wasn't ready yet, so I continued to beat my face. Fifteen minutes later, I was ready. I stood in the mirror to check my outfit out. Damn, I looked good and was ready to have a good time with Three. I had a good feeling about this one, but before placing my phone inside my clutch, I called an Uber so I could meet him at the 7Eleven.

The Uber didn't take any time to arrive. I got in the back seat and introduced myself to the driver. He drove for about five minutes and was pulling up to the spot. I thanked my Uber driver and exited the car. Three wasn't there yet, so I decided to go inside the store and get a few items. I grabbed a Figi bottle water and some mints and proceeded towards the counter. Waiting on the cashier to ring me up, I felt a breeze on the back of my neck. I turned around, and Three was standing there in all black.

"I guess great minds think alike, sir," I said.

"You got that right, baby," he responded.

"$4.50," the cashier said.

Three pulled out his wallet and handed the man one five dollar bill. "Keep the change. I'm ready for my lady, if you don't mind," Three said to the cashier.

The cashier smiled and placed the change in the loose change tray.

Three walked me to my side of the car and opened my door. I got in slowly, just enough to show him my legs and ankles.

"Damn, lady. You are so beautiful."

"Thank you," I responded as he shut the door.

He opened his door and got in. Looking over at me he said, "How would you feel if we go grab dinner and then head back to my spot?" he asked.

"I was looking forward to going dancing. I love to dance, and you promised me," I responded only to avoid going to his house. It wasn't the right time.

"That's absolutely fine, young lady. I know the perfect spot to take you."

"Say no more, let's get going."

He started up his Mercedes Benz E 300 Sedan, and it purred so smooth. So smooth, it had me drift off for a second, day dreaming of the day I would be behind the wheel of such a sexy car. As I was coming back from day dreaming, Three asked, "What's on your mind?"

"Thinking of the day I will be able to have a car like this. One of my own," I responded.

"Is that right? I know if you were my lady, you would get anything you like, including a car such as this, but I don't want you thinking I'm moving too fast," he responded.

"Game on point," I said.

"Baby girl, I know there's an age difference, but know this, I don't ever play games. I go for what I want, and you, ma'am, are what I want."

"Let's see how tonight goes, and we can pick up this conversation later," I said.

After driving for about an hour, we pulled up to Charlene's. A popular lounge by the beach where you could hear live music and dance. I'd been here before with another sponsor. He pulled up to valet parking and handed the man the keys and then walked over to my side and opened the door. He grabbed my right hand and helped me out the car.

"Mmm...Mmm...Mmm. I can't wait to get my hands on all that," he said.

"You'll get your chance, be patient," I responded.

As we walked up to the door, he already had our names down, so the hostess walked us to our VIP section. So far, Three was working to be the top sponsor of the month. I felt my phone vibrate in my purse. I knew it was only Marisa asking me if I would need her. I decided to let it go to voice mail. She was going to be get upset, but she'd get over it.

We had a few drinks before the band took a break, and the DJ took over. The first song he played was one of my favorites, Tank –When We. With liquor in my system and the song feeling good on me, I got on the dance floor and pulled him with me. I started winding my hips from left to right as I swung my hair and bent over to show him just how much rhythm I had in me. Before the middle of the song came on, he was rock hard and standing at attention.

"You like, Daddy?" I asked.

"Hell yeah. You know what you don', huh?"

He grabbed my waist and pulled me into him more and leaned in to whisper in my ear, "Can I have you?"

"We'll see," I responded.

"I want you now, please."

As soon as he said please, I knew I had him right where I wanted him. Now it was time for me to go in for the kill. I turned around, looked him in his eyes, and said, "Let's get out of here."

We walked off the dance floor, walked over to our table, and picked up our belongings and headed towards the front door. He handed the valet the ticket stub with a twenty dollar bill. They returned the car within minutes. We got in, and he started driving to his house. I pulled out my phone and text Marisa that I would be staying over his house for the night but would be back in the morning. She texted me back, "Be careful. I love you, girl."

Chapter Eight

Marisa

    I was glad me and my bestie were making money to get out of our situation. After Antonio broke my heart, I was done with love, or so I thought. After graduation, I just wanted money, nice clothes, jewelry, and the finer things in life. I was skeptical at first about dating older guys for money, but that quickly went away when I found out how much they were willing to pay and the nice places they would take me.

    But lately, things had been getting a little difficult. I was gaining feelings for one of my dates, and I think he shared the same feelings. I never kept a secret from my best friend before, but KJ was really pulling my heart strings; he was the nicest out of all my daddy's. I giggled to myself thinking about when Me'chelle started referring to our dates as that, considering hers was an asshole, and I didn't have a clue who mine was.

Tonight, I was going to the movies and an after-hours coffee house with KJ because last night he was a little upset that I wasn't available. Even though I was feeling him, he didn't need to know all my business. I looked at the time and realized it was almost nine, and we were going to the eleven o'clock show to see Proud Mary. I got up and gathered my things to take a shower and headed to the bathroom. I loved taking long, hot showers, but I still had to do my hair, shave, and get dressed. I wanted to look good for my boo tonight. I had plans for him tonight; he just didn't know it yet.

When I walked out the bathroom, I bumped dead into Antonio. Yes, you heard me correctly; he was still living here just barely. I rolled my eyes and smacked my lips.

"Damn, watch where you're going" I barked and tried to pass him before going into my room, but he cornered me in the bathroom by putting his hands on both sides of the wall.

"Marisa, why are you acting like that? I told you I was sorry I hurt you, but you won't let me explain," he said.

"You damn right, because I wasn't interested in your explanation then, and I'm still not, now please get out my way, I have a date," I spat.

"A date? Who are you going out with?" he questioned. I chuckled a little at his jealousy that was clearly written all over his face.

"Somebody that's not cheating on me, other than that fact, none of your damn business."

Before I knew it, he grabbed me and kissed me. I don't know what came over me, but I kissed him back with so much passion. I quickly came to my senses though and pushed him away.

I hurried past him leaving him standing there looking stupid. What fuck he thought this was? I'm not someone he can use when he gets ready, I thought as I closed my door and locked it. I went to my closet and pulled out my black one-piece bodysuit, my tan blazer, and tan pumps. I lotioned my body with my Victoria Secret Pure Seduction, followed by the body spray and put on my clothes. I unwrapped my hair and let it fall to my shoulders. I applied my Mac makeup lightly with some lip gloss, looked myself over in the mirror to make sure my booty and boobs looked right in this outfit, and by then, my phone was ringing. I knew by the Trey Songz ringtone Love Faces, that it was KJ, and a smile broke through. "Hello," I answered in my sexy voice.

"Hey beautiful, I'm pulling in your complex now," he said.

"Okay, see you in a minute," I replied. I grabbed my purse, a few hundred out my secret hiding spot, and left out my room. Antonio was sitting in the living room smoking a blunt looking like a lost puppy when I passed by. I didn't say a word, putting an extra twist in my step so he could see what he was missing. You could call me petty or whatever, but I did kind of wonder where his Mrs. Perfect was and why he came home tonight after being gone for weeks. I heard a horn blow jarring me out my thoughts. Oh well, that was none of my business anyway.

I walked out the door and down the steps to KJ's grey and black Dodge Charger. We both started smiling as soon as we saw each other. I walked around to the passenger seat and got in giving him a hello kiss and hug. Umm...he looks and smells so good as usual, I thought as he pulled off in the direction of the theater. I asked him how his day was, and if he was still mad at me for canceling on him the night before. He said he wasn't, but I knew better. Not wanting to get in a big discussion about why I couldn't make it, I turned up the radio and sat back to clear my head.

Fifteen minutes later, we pulled up to the theater, and it was a long line just like I knew it would be, but it was moving kind of fast. He parked as close as possible, and we got out and walked. I was dreading waiting in line with these heels on, but when he grabbed my hand and walked me straight through the door and to the concession stand, I knew something was up, but I wasn't going to speak on it. We ordered our refreshments and went straight in the showing room. There was an usher standing there in his red jacket. KJ showed him something, but it wasn't a ticket I'm sure, and he told us to go on in. I hadn't been to the movie theater since they remolded it years ago, and since then they had put small tables in there to put your food and drinks on. We found a good seat in the middle where no one else was around and sat down. A few minutes later, the lights dimmed, and the previews began to play. KJ reached over to hold my hand. I'm not going to lie, it sent a tingle through my body, and it felt good, but for some reason, I couldn't get my mind off of Antonio.

We watched the movie and, it was good. Taraj P Henson was such a great actress. While everyone else rushed to get out, we stayed in our seat and talked waiting for them to go out. He asked if I was excited about going to the coffee house for the first time, I said yes, but I wasn't really focused on that. After about ten minutes, we finally got up to leave, and we walked to the car. I felt my phone vibrate in my purse, so I looked at it and realized I had a couple of text messages. One was from Me'chelle saying that she decided to go home; she would tell me why later and to call her. The other three were from Antonio saying that he really needed to talk to me and that he didn't know who this new dude was, but he couldn't love me like he did and to just hear him out. I was so stuck reading I didn't even realize I was standing in the middle of the parking lot while KJ was already unlocking the doors of the car.

I texted him back saying I would see him in a couple of hours and stuck my phone back in my purse.

"Is everything okay?" he questioned.

I gave a fake smile and told him yes and that my mom wasn't feeling too good so I couldn't stay too long at the club.

"I was hoping you could spend the night with me," he said with a visible attitude. "Look Marisa, I don't know what's going on with you, but there are plenty of women that would enjoy my time, and I'm here trying to spend it with you, and you brushin' me off like I'm some kind of lame or somethin'!" he yelled at me.

"KJ, it's not that at all. I really do need to see about my mom," I lied. "How about we go on a double date tomorrow; me, you, my bestie, and her dude? We can all go to the club together."

"Naw, I don't chill with no dudes I don't know; you can bring your friend if you want, and I will bring my brother," he said nonchalantly.

"Okay, it's a date," I said as he turned around in the gas station to take me home. I felt my phone vibrating again. I had an idea who it was, but it probably wasn't a good time to check it; I was on my way home anyway.

Twenty minutes later, we pulled up in front of my house, and I saw Tell and Antonio standing on the porch talking.

"Who the fuck is that at your house?" KJ asked looking intensely up on the porch.

"Oh, that's my mom's boyfriend and his brother; he came over until I got here," I explained.

"Oh, yeah? Hey, let me get your friend's number so she can talk to my brother about the date tomorrow. You still comin', right?"

"Yes, of course." I gave him Me'chelle's number.

"Tell her his name is Clint; he will call her tonight probably," he said. "Okay baby, give me a kiss with your sexy ass," he said so sweetly.

I leaned in giving him a kiss. I really didn't want to in front of Tell and Antonio's nosey asses, but I also didn't want KJ thinking I was with one of them. He seemed to have a little jealous streak, but I thought it was cute. We hugged, and I went upstairs to my apartment. I waved, and he blew the horn before speeding off.

Antonio and Tell were looking at me like I was growing horns.

"Marisa, was that KJ in that car?" Antonio asked me, shocking the hell out of me.

"Yes, it was, and how do you know his name?" I asked.

"So, your date was with one of the biggest pimps in town with your green ass?" Antonio said pissing me off.

"KJ is not no pimp, asshole. You just jealous because I'm not fucking you no more," I retorted before storming in the house to call my bestie, Me'chelle. I hated liars, and I was really going to hear him out until he lied on my boo.

Chapter Nine

Me'Chelle

      This was the night. I decided that after my date with Three, I was going back to his place and give him a night he would never forget. We've been on a few dates, and each of them I ended up leaving right before things got too heated. I knew I was teasing, and each time it pissed him off more and more. I mean daddy, as I started calling him, was spending bread on me and the twins. Hell, he was even giving me extra to keep my drunken dad satisfied and out of my business.

I placed the black and red nighty with the matching thong I bought at Victoria Secret's last week in my overnight bag. "Daddy would love to see me in this," I said to myself.

My ringtone, "Dat's my main one. Dat's my main one. Yeah, she up in here with me right now," started going off letting me know Marisa was calling me.

"Hey girl, what's up?" I answered.

"What you up to?" she asked.

"Getting ready for Daddy."

"Ok. Call me when you can. Antonio just pissed me off, but I can tell you later. Be careful," she said.

"You sure?"

"Yeah, call me later."

"Ok. I'll make sure to call you as soon as I get back in the morning."

"Ok, girl."

I knew my girl was falling for her sponsor KJ, but at the same time, I thought she would never get over Antonio's cheating ass. Hearing the agitated tone in her voice when she mentioned his name, told me I was wrong. Risa had been through so much, and she didn't deserve any more heartaches in her life, and Antonio broke her down. I was happy my girl was getting over his hoe ass.

After hanging up with Marisa, I felt a need that I should go be with her. I picked up my phone and called Three.

"Hey, beautiful," he answered.

"Hi, daddy. Would you mind if I took a rain check on tonight's plans?" I asked.

"Is everything ok?" he asked.

"With me? Yes, daddy. I have a strong feeling that I need to go be with Marisa. She just called me, and I didn't like how she sounded. I promise, I'll make it up to you."

"When are you leaving to go see her?" he asked.

"I was just about to hop in the shower before she called. I would say about an hour."

"Ok, Chelle, my bell," he said. "I'll be seeing you."

"Thank you, daddy."

I went to the bathroom and hopped in the shower, washed up, and got out. I put on my ripped jeans with a white v-neck shirt and my all white Air Max. Wanting to surprise Marisa, I grabbed my overnight bag and placed another outfit in the bag. No nighty tonight, so I folded it back up and put it in my bottom drawer.

I walked down the hallway and checked on the twins and proceeded out the door. The street light on my block was out, which made it extra dark. I started walking towards Marisa's house. As I turned the corner, I saw a car I recognized. I thought to myself, Why, would he be over here? No, that can't be him.

Ring ....ring. My phone started going off. I started to pull my phone from out of my purse when all of a sudden everything went black. Someone muffled my mouth and placed a bag over my head, picked me up, and threw me in the trunk. My heart was beating fast, and I couldn't scream. All I could think about were the twins. What are they going to do without me? I tried to remove the bag from my head by wiggling but then I felt another body next to me. The body was moving. The more I thought about there being a dead body next to me, the more I freaked out. I felt the car stop. I heard footsteps walk to the trunk, but they didn't open it. They got back in the car and started driving.

Lanes of Love

What am I going to do now? How will I get out of this situation? Who is the other person next to me? Are they alive? All these questions ran through my head. I just laid there thinking and ended up falling asleep.

"Help, help," I heard the person next to me saying. The last help sent shivers up my spine. If I wasn't mistaken, that was Marisa's voice.

Marisa, Marisa, I tried to say, but the only thing I could get out was "Mmmmmmm.mmmmmm."

The car stopped, and then the trunk opened………

To be continued……

Soulja Choc Presents Authors

Play to Win

By:

Tosha Dodd-Dunnaville

Chapter One
What a fool

      My favorite day of the year will be here in seven days, but I can't shake the feeling something isn't right with my one and only sweetheart. I've known him almost my entire life. We met in my first year of high school and I have been head over heels in love with him since the first time I laid eyes on him. We got engaged our senior year in high school. My now fiancée has been everything to me since freshman year of high school, but lately that man hasn't been the person I have known and love, although he is my world. I will give him anything he wants, all he has to do is ask, and I'll make it happen. Truthfully, he doesn't even have to ask, I have his back no matter what.

It's been a while since he has had a job so it strikes me as odd that he has been super busy lately. I call him from my place of work every shift that I am scheduled and my plea for his company falls on deaf ears with him. It's my dream to build a life with him. I mean I want a family. I'm talking two kids, maybe even three, a dog, and a house with a white picket fence and a two car garage. I'm supportive of him being back in school because having a college degree will benefit us both, not to mention it was my idea to begin with. I have my degree as a Registered Nurse.

I plan to go back to school next year to further my academic career to become a Physician Assistant. I just want my man to execute his plan first. I can't put my finger on what's going on but I know it's something. I mean I told him I loved him last night and he said, "Right back at ya babe" like it was comical before he left to take care of whatever business goes down at 10pm. Those simple words cut like a knife. I guess it's going to be a long work day for me again, and before I knew it just like that I was back at work again.

"Hi, are you Candice?" I asked my uncomfortable impatient patient waiting on the hospital bed in one of the raggedy hospital gowns that we provide.

"Isn't that what the chart you just accessed said?" She asked sarcastically tilting her big bobble head to the side and rolling her eyes.

It took everything I had not to slap her mouth shut. She had lips so big that the song duck tales started playing in my head as her theme song. I ignored her ignorance, handed her the cup to fill with urine, and showed her where the bathroom was after letting her know that she would be tested for pregnancy. She came in complaining of back pain so the doctor took her as a drug seeker and asked me to test her for pregnancy before he came in to find out her cocktail preference. Sadly, people with real pain do not get properly treated because those with pretend pain make it harder on everybody else. It wasn't long before the handsome Dr. Franklin himself and I went together to tell her that she is pregnant. My heart broke for her as she sat there crying her heart out.

I wish there was a baby growing inside of me. Immediately, it was clear that they were not tears of joy. Dr. Franklin shot me a glance of please talk to her. I nodded and pulled up a stool to listen to Candice. She didn't need me to talk, she needs someone to listen. "I don't even know him; I mean not really, not enough for this. He says he wants me forever but like this though?" I didn't say anything. "We just started hooking up a few weeks ago." she turned her phone around to show me a video and there she was on her knees in an isolated parking lot. I couldn't believe how this beautiful girl has no respect for herself.

I couldn't see the man at first but as the video played on, I watched the man that picked her up, put her on the trunk of the car, and fucked her like his life depended on that next nut show his face. The same face that swears to love only me was right there being recorded by God knows who. Before I knew it my new mascara was all down my face. My tears were not tears of joy either. I knew the man in the video. He was mines. My fiancé, Damien Rowland Carter confirmed my gut wrenching fear that things have changed. I knew things had changed but this is someone I dedicated my whole life to. I never pictured him shattering my soul like this. What hurts the most is he engaged in sex with a woman he doesn't even know unprotected.

It made matters worse when her phone rang with Damien's face popping up on the caller id. I'm standing here in pain and he is calling her. I can't believe he was calling her. Candice didn't notice my tears when she took the video call.

"Hey Candy Cane." She just looked at her Galaxy 8 note. "Are you at the hospital?" He asked seeing her ensemble.

I walked behind her quietly and stood where he could see me, because I wanted him to see me, know I need him to see me. He really fucked up this time so he hung up real quick. He hung up so quick that I am not sure God himself saw him push the red end call button. I wanted to choke this trick but she doesn't know who I am. She had my man in a way only meant for me or supposed to be. She enjoyed what is mine all too well. I have to stay calm and remember she knows really knows nothing about me like at all. We both got lied to. He is so selfish for this. I am his woman and I deserve to be treated like somebody. All of the time I have spent on him feels wasted.

"I guess we lost signal." She said ignorant to all facts.

She hopped off the table, quickly got dressed, and took her discharge papers never noticing my pain. I think I am going to leave early today; I am going to have to, because I can't help any patient that comes in here today with my own injury being to this degree. Woman down, I need back up. What a fool. My man clearly doesn't love me anymore. I really thought he still did. I know that her phone didn't lose signal. He hung up. What will he say to this? What can he say to me? What will he say to her? I need answers to all of this right now. All I ever wanted from him is to be loved for who I am. I guess I asked for too much.

Candice came back catching me and my thoughts off guard. I forgot to give her the script that Dr. Franklin printed out for her before she left. She wanted her prenatal vitamins. This girl seemed so full of herself that it made me sick. Well, it looks like she is keeping it.

"Are you okay Nurse Mila?" She asked me.

The kindness and concern in her voice shocked me because she was so rude earlier.

"I just got some life changing news." I said.

"That makes two of us." She joked.

Little did she know that her news was our news.

"I am about to go and call Damien to let him know we are about to be a family." I felt like she punched me.

"I thought you didn't know him."

She looked around the empty room. I stayed seated in front of the computer I was noting her chart on.

She explained, "We met online after we both went through a bad break up. My whole life just turned into a nightmare. We talked online for months. We met in person a few weeks ago. The sexual chemistry is everything. I just don't know him as a person." I swallowed my tears. She thanked me for listening and rushed away to get to Damien's call. Despite being me in the video chat unknown to her, he was calling her again. I cannot believe this mess. He is calling her from the phone I bought him. He was calling her from our rental home that I pay for every month. He did not call or text me. Yeah, I am definitely going to be leaving work right after I finish updating her chart. I am going to make him face me.

While I'm already in her chart, let me just read her history, and memorize her personal information. It's a great asset to have a photographic memory. Damn, this isn't even her first pregnancy. She had a child last year; thank God there is no history of sexually transmitted diseases. I mean she literally just had a baby last year, and I've been trying to get pregnant by Damien for a year now then here comes this Candice girl he even nicknamed giving him something he was supposed to want with me. I really do honestly wonder what his response to this news will be. I'm super irritated right now. What happened? I just can't grasp this right now. I'm so damn mad, hurt, sad, and irritated. I would go bust the windows out his car but that's mine too. I bought him that car for his birthday last year. I got the car he wanted for him but never put it in his name. I am a procrastinator and in this case, that's to my benefit. I mean, I also saw myself as being his wife so I figured who cares if the car is in my name or his. It makes no difference. I feel less than a woman right now. I feel like I do not matter. I feel sick too. Have I eaten today? I can't remember.

I met my fiancé in high school about eleven years ago. I didn't even want him at first. He could sing, dance, and was athletic before his injury. I was shy, to myself, basically an introvert. Damien opened me up to a world of no depression, love, laughter, self-confidence, and happiness. As an adult, I am very outgoing, the head emergency room Registered Nurse, and people gravitate towards me. I don't know if me working all of the time sent Damien into the arms of "Candy Cane" but who is going to feed us if I don't?

"Nurse Mila, Earth to Mila!" Dr. Franklin stood looking like a steak dinner. Good God, he is extra fine today. "Are you okay?"

I nodded but my flooded face told him the truth. He told me to go home. Dr. Franklin is kind, always professional, and clearly attractive but I would never have cheated on Damien. I have heard that some of the doctors including Dr. Franklin have asked about me. Damien is the only love that I have ever had. The only person I've ever been with at all is Damien. I wonder if my refusal to lick his stick sent him to Candice. She has no idea who I am outside of being her nurse for a few hours but the truth will come to light. It always does. Just like me, she is clueless, but eventually, the light will turn on for her too.

I thanked Dr. Franklin and headed down the road to the employee parking lot where my Chrysler Aspen spent every day waiting for me. I call her Charlotte. The walk is usually about five minutes long but today took what felt like five ages. At least two canes and walkers passed me by. I know that I should be going home to tell Damien to get out but instead I want to talk about how to work it out. I hope Candice told him because I cannot share patient information. The last job he had was taking in recycled cans. I am not sure what occupation that qualifies as maybe Canman, hell I don't know. I believe in him so I have supported his unemployed life and encouraged his college plan. He keeps changing curriculums so I have no idea what he is taking right now, I just cannot keep up.

***

About That Home Life

Takes more than a house to make a home

    Damien's car was gone. He probably went to talk to Candice about the news. Candice Grace Phillips. She lives right around the corner. How convenient for him. I took in a breath and parked on the yard. I want to get inside my house before Mrs. Parker comes out asking me for free healthcare. I made it to the door when I heard the old woman yell for me. I did not respond. I pretended that I did not hear her. I opened the door to my home and went right back outside to check the house numbers because everything I owned was gone. Damien's stuff was gone too. We have been robbed. I cannot believe it.

    I ran to Mrs. Parkers to call the police, because my phone was dead. She laughed at my panic and told me she saw mover's earlier taking things out the house. She asked if I forgot I was moving. The only one who moved was Damien. I was not even worth a goodbye. He robbed me of everything including my pride. I can't believe this. I can replace everything but him. I asked Mrs. Parker to use her phone. She approved my request. I called Damien but the phone went straight to his voicemail. How convenient for him. I thanked Mrs. Parker, said goodnight to her after thirty minutes of listening to her go on about her hemorrhoid, I finally made my escape. Mr. Parker was asleep in his lazy boy. Thank God for that. Damien owed me an explanation. He broke our home.

***

Photographic Memory

Candice Grace Phillips

26 yr. old Caucasian female

9021 Hank Lane

  I drove less than two minutes before pulling up to Candice's shoe box sized apartment. There was Damien sitting outside with her on his lap. They were taking selfies. I was close enough to be seen but remained unnoticed. The car I bought him right off the lot was parked in front of her place. She is beautiful, despite her bobble head that was the resemblance of a Bratz doll, and mountain mouth. Candice is a fiery red head with emerald green eyes. She is number two because I was here first. Man, her smile is intoxicating. I read in her chart that she is a physical therapist so why does she live here? Damien and his little Mrs. Number Two, Wait! They are sitting on my wicker loveseat. I saved an entire month for that wicker set. My phone charged a little from my car port. I wasn't going to do it but my broken heart led me to report the car stolen. Damien did not pay for a dog on thing but there he was happily enjoying my things with her. I went as far as to tell the 911 operator that I can see my car and it did not take long at all for the police to roll up and shut down their little party of two. I saw no signs of the child that her records said she birthed last year.

  I watched the police talk to Damien and despite not being able to hear them, I knew it was about my car. I felt bad but he even took my phone charger. What did I do to deserve this kind of treatment? I could tell my name sounded familiar to Candice when the officers mentioned it. She was deep in thought the second she saw Damien drop his head. Damien was handcuffed and escorted to the police car. I started my

Chrysler Aspen up right before they put him in the back of the police car. He saw me, Candice did too, and after looking from one of their faces to the others face. I focused on Damien. The arresting officer put him in his car so I pulled off after seeing that she added up why my name was familiar.

I knew she would because she was clearly thinking hard when she went inside her apartment to get my car keys to hand over to the cops who gave the keys to a tow truck driver. I stayed anonymous to the police. I had no place to sleep at home and I mean that literally. I mean the entire house is completely empty like no life was ever there. I took my broken heart to Comfort Inn and checked into a room as lonely old me. I have no family. My parents died in the nine eleven catastrophe. I have no friends because I am always at work. All of my contacts are work related. I should pray but right now, I just can't. I feel so empty and void. My phone went off shaking me from thoughts of my needed prayers.

***

You have a free call from Roanoke City jail......do you accept?

Unfortunate phone call

Damien

"Hello." It was noisy in the background. "Mila." Damien said my name like today didn't happen.

I wanted to forgive him and forget this.

"Mila, are we doing this?" I laughed but it wasn't because I felt amused.

"Damien, I want to know why?" He took a deep breath.

"Mila I wasn't happy anymore." I interrupted him.

"You were not happy to be loved, cared for, protected, and accepted?" He took another deep breath.

"Loving you was easy when we were in high school. I never meant to hurt you. I am sorry."

I want to believe him but this is what Layton calls jail talk, which is when incarcerated people is filling your head up with lies of love. She stays at work talking about one gangsta or another. She actually educated me to something called, Game.

"Damien, I did not deserve that and I know you're not sorry. You just want to get out of jail."

There went another deep breath. I feel like I can't breathe "Mila. I didn't steal the car. You know it was a gift. I've been soaking in pain for so long that Candice became my medication by simple conversation. It was innocent." I listened. "I took her in small doses, a little more, and then we got hooked." I wouldn't be able to talk between the tears and pain in my chest if I tried so I just listened to Damien silently trying to regain my composure. "I tried to talk to you but no, you always had to go, and there I was alone again hoping you would see how empty I felt because you wouldn't listen to me not even for a minute, and there are twenty four hours in each day, that's for sure. I heard all about your day but mine never mattered. I fucked up Mila but I lost you long before I left." I just held the phone crying.

"I am not perfect Damien. I regret not listening to you. I know it's no excuse but I'm human. I never saw this coming. I really didn't. I just wanted to secure the bag for our future." Damien waited for a minute then started talking again.

"Mila, I'm tired. I waited on our Stars to align but they didn't so here we are at the truth. I want you to be able to handle it though." I sobbed uncontrollably. I would never be ready for this. "Mila, I love you but I am in love with Candice. I don't know what happened but she is magic. She never complicates things. I bumped into her out the blue online and before I knew it, I wasn't mad anymore."

The truth really does hurt because my broken heart just left my body.

"I tried to give us a happy and secured home Damien. I wanted to be your wife. We are engaged. Life is mean. I'm in love with you but you want that piece of trash. She met up with you like the secret she was." Damien didn't say anything for a second. The phone hung up but he called back to continue our conversation. I guess more so to continue our separation or break up. I am hoping he just needs a little time. I don't want this. I want him to fight with me for us.

"I meant you no harm Mila. Our journey has ended. Our season is over. Candice makes me feel like I'm home no matter where we are. She came through for me bringing straight light when I was in a very dark place." I thought about the baby, the video, and wanted to scream at him but I couldn't, because of the HIPPA law. I will not share patient information.

"Mila, I am sorry I hurt you, but I can't apologize for choosing Candice." The tears poured down my eyes so hard that it hurt my soul to the core. I thought Damien loved me but he just fucked up my whole life. I've been carrying a bottle of Klonopin around for ages. I took a few to calm my nerves all of the way down. I can never hate this man but I'm going to drop my truth on him too.

"You think my boss didn't look tempting Damien? He did, and still does but I love you, and respect us. I hold the hands of abused people including children contemplating suicide and you forgot about me and my sacrifice for us when you turned to a stranger. I struggled through school but I never complained, because I saw people who had it worse than me so I prayed and held on. He started to speak. "No, you got to bleed so it's my turn to tell my story. I neglected you but it was because I was trying to secure us. I asked God to keep me focused. You think I like going through the drama with your Momma? No matter what, I made it happen, and I never folded. You wouldn't be able to walk a mile in my shoes but we all have a situation. You owed me an explanation and as fucked up as it is, you got me good. You lied to me and her but you love us? Nigga, you love you. I was on your team. I hope when you tell her about me you tell her about everything you took before her, during her, and now with her. Tell her how I busted my ass to feed us. You'll never find another me Damien but you'll search for me in everybody you meet. While we are on the subject of you telling her about me, let me tell you about you. You better be glad I didn't get pregnant. You better be glad we never said I do. I mean, what's it take to be appreciated? You said our journey is over so I'm going to wish you the best of luck inmate. You didn't steal my car but you took everything I own but my Aspen and clothes on my back." He told me he wanted me to feel as empty as he did before her.

"I get it Damien. You want Candace. You're in love. If it wasn't for bad luck, I wouldn't have any. I lost both my parents but still pray for peace every day. There's a message in this madness. I'm not going to ask you to stay with me. You're so blind right now because you can't see past yourself. I forgive you because I know that you don't see what you're doing to yourself. You don't care what you're doing to me. Holidays will come and they will feel different without you but I'll still light the tree. Someday I'll do it with a beautiful baby of my own. I'm not giving up on being loved because you gave up on me, "Nah" I don't give up on me. I'm going to keep my head up and continue to call on my God. I appreciate you taking all of my stuff because there's no trace of you left to see. Hear me and hear me well because after today I don't know you. I never knew you. Who knew the last time we were together it would be the last time? Again, I apologize to you because I didn't listen, but I'm too good of a woman to deserve this. I'm top of the line. I thank God that I can't turn back the time because our whole life was a lie. You're going to miss me baby, but I'm gone." I threw my phone across the room and faced reality.

It's time for me to come around and find a new approach to an old dream. I'll be better without him then I ever was with him. Lord I don't know what to blame for this pain, but let's go into my next chapter together. God, let Jesus take wheel because I do not know how to get there alone.

Where's home now? If only clicking one's heels worked

I slept a few hours. Thank God for that. I feel better than expected. I need to go get a replacement phone and a new number. I was shocked to see that the man who checked me out was Dr. Franklin. He looks so different outside of scrubs and lab coats. Dr. Franklin didn't pry but we did exchange enough chit chat for me to discover that he owns the hotel. It's a family business. The man is impressive. I can tell by his face that he enjoys having a busy life. I also learned that he is single with no children. God is good. I decided to ask the good doctor to dinner. We agreed to meet at Cheddars at seven o'clock tonight. There is no replacing what Damien and I had, but I sure can upgrade it. Hmmm Dinner with the doctor

"Nurse" He smiled himself into another gear. "Mila thank you for this. It's long overdue." I smiled.

"Overdue?" He smiled back and responded,

"I've wanted to ask you out for the past three years now." He just made my whole day better.

I learned so much about him. For starters his name is Samuel. He has an allergy to cherries, but it is interesting that cherry is his favorite flavor. Samuel is a Vikings fan, my Dad was too, and just like me, he enjoys swimming. The conversation went on so long that the waitress had to tell us they were closing soon and then she came back a little while after to tell us that they were closed. We were not ready to end the night but we did. I had so much fun that the pain I felt from Damien did not hurt. The pain from Damien never even crossed my mind until it was time go home to no bed. I took a gamble and checked back into the Comfort Inn. A young white male checked me in. I was hoping to see Samuel again.

I don't understand how Damien could just up and go like that. I hope he finds everything he wanted. I put it on my life that I never saw this coming. I kept it loyal with him since high school, never once deceived him, and I can't be the only one to have ever loved that hard or that long, but I refuse to let what we went through put me through so much depression that I lose myself. I never asked for perfection because we were perfect to me. It's sick how he compared his new love thang to me. I never did go get me another phone. I used the hotel phone to check my messages. Damien called and it wasn't from jail. I will drop charges but I am taking that car to the women's shelter and giving it to the first person who walks out to the bus stop with a child first thing tomorrow morning. It's a Mustang so not a family car but it's free with no lien.

Candice called asking for a woman to woman talk. I have nothing to say. Samuel called too. I smiled. "Mila, this evening was nice. Thank you. I was hoping to talk to you but okay, good night." I played it back a few times. Dr. Samuel Franklin grew up in Salem, Virginia in a two parent home. He lost his mother to breast cancer and his father has Alzheimer's. I know that's hard but he was not telling me a sob story. Samuel is a success story. I would never have thought him to be single, so put together in his personal life, and I really enjoyed his company. I am looking forward to seeing him again. I let thirty minutes pass me by before I called my line back to get Samuel's number.

I called him. "Dr. Franklin. This is Nurse Mila. Hi." I was not sure what he would say because it's late.

"Mila hi you are here? Me too" I smiled so big he had to hear it. "Come to my room." I had to tell him hold on because there was a knock at the door. It was him. Samuel. I hugged him so tight. He looked at my naked body. I forgot I was naked but he seemed to enjoy the view. He smiled and pulled me back into him when I went to grab a robe. He smells so good. I wanted him to stay so I asked him to lay with me tonight. He held me closer then picked me up like he was carrying me over the threshold. He kicked the door shut behind him being careful with me in his arms then there we were lying on the bed holding each other. He was a gentleman. I asked him to play some music. He put on some Ciara. The song played and I sang along. It was comforting to me for him to fall asleep holding me. I wanted him so bad but it's not the time to take it there. Something about him put my heart back together. I want to love him. I believe his actions. He has not even tried to kiss me but I know we both wanted that and more. I know that I sure wanted more to happen.

Chapter Two

Work

    I slept very well despite the pinch my heart feels waking up to an empty room. Samuel was gone and I had to be at work. I hope seeing each other outside of work do not make work uncomfortable. I walked in to Layton telling me there were tulips delivered, my favorite flower. I picked up my purple tulips and smelled them. The card read, "Thank-you for walking into my life. Samuel." The other nurses were green with envy. I turned around to see Damien standing there. The look on his face seeing those tulips in my hand was priceless.

"Can we talk?" he asked.

I could see Samuel looking at us. I nodded to avoid a scene. I know Damien and he will not accept know for an answer. I took him into the break room.

"Nice tulips." I did not hide my happiness.

"I know." he looked distraught.

"I am busy, Damien." he looked around, shut the door, and watched me admire my tulips. I did not even look at him.

"I do love you, Mila." I really was not trying to hear nothing from him at all. Damien was my prince charming. I will always love him but I never saw that knife coming. I really didn't. The trust is gone. I wanted to make what we had worked, I wanted to forgive him, but he told me he chose his candy.

"Damien, I said everything I needed to say." I kept looking at my tulips. The vase alone looks more expensive than my vehicle alone.

"Mila" he called while I'm still looking at my flowers.

"I am listening Damien. I excused the charges this morning. The car will be re-gifted." he made some moan of disapproval. I don't even care anymore what he thinks. I tried my best.

"I did not expect you to be so chirpy." I looked him in his eyes. "I cried my tears Damien. I cried until it hurt me to my soul. I will not continue that spree. What do you want? You want to see me cry for the rest of my life behind you? You took everything including my pride. You tore down the private hell you yourself told me I had you living in. I will not put up a fight. I cannot believe that this is my life but it is and despite the side effects of being depressed inside, I am good. Nothing is worth my happiness, not even you. I forgive you but I will never forget this." Damien locked eyes with me. He was crying. "I thought we were stronger than this

Damien." he shook his head. I looked back at my tulips to keep from crying again. I did what I could to survive with him. I never knew I had the strength to accept a change but I really am good.

Layton came in and turned right back around realizing the break room was too serious at the moment.

"Damien, I am always going to remember every Valentine you ever gave me but you need to go." I felt the fire from his face splash me. I will not look at him again.

"Candice….." I stopped him. "I can give a tea about Candice. You are not messing my day up. Step back Satan."

"Mila I am in love with you. Candice told me she is not keeping it because if I can hurt you she knows I can hurt her."

I smiled at last night but responded. "My love never again will I lower my standards. You disrespected me. I have nothing to say to you not even about Candice. You said you want to leave so go." Damien stepped towards me. I moved.

"Mila let me make this up to you." Damien took a knee and asked my hand in marriage with a ring I am sure that I paid for.

"Damien, get up. Just go." he stayed on that knee, the same right knee that he injured in a football game.

I don't know why but I thought about New Years and the anger inside me spoke with the pain. "Letting go is not easy Damien. I can't believe you have the audacity to even be here lying to my face because Candice decided she wanted everything I had but you. I will write it all off as a donation on my taxes. You really thought what I needed right now is a fake ass marriage proposal." I laughed angrily. "This is just making the pain exceedingly more painful. I hope you find everything you need to make you happy but me, I am just Mila. I am just someone you use to know." I have to let God help him climb the mountain he put himself on.

He will never win if he never even tries. Like he said himself, our season has ended." The road won't be easy and he will suffer trials but hope is not gone with God. I walked away still holding my tulips.

Samuel was still standing in the same spot. I told him all about Damien, my pain, Candice, and how I am afraid to move into anything serious anytime soon. Last night was serious, we both felt it, and nothing is being forced. Samuel is not just a doctor; he is a publisher, and a damn good one at that. I took a look at his books and the work of his authors and I am very impressed. Everything about Samuel tells me that there is so much more in life left for me to learn. I know we have to keep it professional but Samuel gave me peace when I almost lost it all mentally. I turned to a pill bottle which can lead to dependency. If you need something, take it, but not to the point of it being a crutch. I am not perfect but I can be perfectly happy. I looked at Samuel the publisher, hotel owner, and took it upon myself to go ease his mind.

"Thank you, Samuel." he looked hurt.

"Absolutely I see you worked everything out." He was really hurt. I looked behind me to see Damien watching us. I turned back to Samuel. "I did. Thanks to you." he looked at me through the peace within himself and listened.

"Will you be my Valentine this year?" he smiled flashing those intoxicating dimples. He nodded and shocked me by taking the vase of tulips out of my hands, placing them on the nurses station, and pulling me in for the kiss we have both been wanting.

"I will be your Valentine for life if you will have me." My entire body felt heaven with his gentle touch, that kiss, and the smell of his cologne alone. I forgot Damien was even there until he walked over to us.

"Never disrespected me, huh?" Samuel looked at him in a way that let him know he could get it. Damien is not about that fighting life. Let me find out Samuel has a little gangsta in him. I like it.

"Damien. Is it? You can see yourself out. I will take Mila from here." Samuel said still holding me but looking at Damien.

Samuel was sly with that rude boy attitude. Real sly and it turned me on. The entire nurse's station was filled with employees confirming Samuel and I. Layton said "Give me my money! I told y'all the day she started working here Dr. Franklin wants that." Samuel and I laughed. We agreed to talk more tonight. We did very well working together. Everyone knew because they are nosey but no one knew the details. Something in his eyes captured my soul. I can see him in my life eternally. I have no unrealistic expectations. We are just going to let it happen naturally.

Chapter Three

Dr. Do Good

Valentine's Day

Today is bittersweet. I love Valentine's Day. People see hearts, flowers, giant sized cards, and all sorts of other things like teddy bears and think it's just an annual review of love. I engage in all of that too but that's not why Valentine's Day is my favorite day of the year. It's my favorite because the history excites me. Let me explain. Don't judge me though. Smiling sarcastically let me educate you before meeting up with what seems to be my Boaz. February the fourteenth, a young Priest who married young couples in secret was executed for what was considered in Rome to be a crime. Can you believe that an actual bloodbath war took place to fight against marriage? Love was frowned upon. Valentine's Day holds a bittersweet story because despite that fact the priest loved love so much that he found it for himself while in jail with the jailer's daughter of all people. Can you imagine being in jail for helping young lovers seal their love with one another for eternity even if it meant doing it in secret? I'm not sure if I would give my freedom for the love of others but for the right love, I would serve life. I really and truly would.

The day of his execution he wrote the jailer's daughter a letter of love and signed it your Valentine before sealing it up. Thinking about the slain warriors made me want to be touched in ways that Valentine's Day is meant for. I love to be choked, teased before pleasure, watching a man stroke his dick always makes me relax into a sensual state of mind. Something about those slain for love just puts me in the mood to be fucked, and hard at that. In my case the only man I've ever seen in action is Damien but tonight I'm going do all of the things I've been dreaming of for years. Damien was very old fashioned. We never fucked, not once, we made love, and it's per his demand that it always had to be in the bedroom. I begged so long to do it on the couch that by the time we got to the bedroom I just lied and said that my period cycle started up so that it would put his dick right on back down. He would say Moses isn't parting the red sea anymore. He used to get all up in it when I was just his girlfriend but things changed when he put a ring on it. I'm glad too that Samuel is only a social drinker because the smell of alcohol really makes my head hurt. Damien smelled so bad when he drank because it was so much that I could smell it through his pores. I've literally become physically sick from that smell.

I need to shift gears because I want to be ready for Samuel. I used my norform last week so my love canal smells like island flowers. Back at the hotel that no longer charged to me I'm waiting patiently in my purple see through silhouette. Just a little decor for what he's already seen. I

Lanes of Love

wanted him that night but I'm glad we waited until my favorite day. Before I knew it Samuel came into the room dressed in a white wife beater and some black sweatpants. I can see all of the blessing God gave him from the print on his sweatpants. Damn. I am in for a treat tonight. I like how Samuel just let himself in. You would never guess there was some gangster in this well rounded man and I like it know that's an understatement I love it. I want all of him and then some more of him. Samuel looked nervous. He was carrying a bear almost as tall as him. We stood about the same height, five feet seven inches tall.

Damien was almost six feet tall. It's strange not looking up. I didn't get him anything. Oh my goodness, oh wait. There is a Meech apparel jogging suit that I bought for Damien but it will fit Samuel. It's in a Valentine's Day gift wrapped packaged too. I'm glad I never had time to stop for Damien a card. There are some Tommy Hilfiger boxer briefs in there too. Covered but before I could say anything Samuel was handing me a robe. I guess I wasn't covering up fast enough because he helped me put it on. This night is not going the way that I planned right now. I should be sucking on his dick right now, which is something I'm not fond of but tonight holds a different mood. I want to hear him go as far as to tell me that I'm his bitch. I want to be his bitch tonight. If he calls me that outside of sexual encounters I might cut him though. I'll be his bitch, slut, and anything else tonight.

I want to try some things Layton talks about at work. There's a position called the doggy style that I would like to be in. Layton also said that the best nut comes when you're on top. I want to see if that's true for me. Samuel picked me up after covering me and took me to the room next door where tulips and matching purple balloons were the main decor. On the floor was a veggie plate equipped with ranch, a steak and shrimp dinner, some lobster, broccoli florets, and non-alcoholic champagne to drink. There was a box of chocolates for dessert. Samuel put me down and pointed at the balloons which all had something written on them. There were fourteen. I was lost. I'm glad I found you. Thank you for you. I have a secret. I'm glad you won't judge. You're beautiful. It's okay to smile. You have a beautiful smile. Pop the question tonight. I'm a virgin. I looked at him then read balloon number ten again. He's a virgin? Like, is he for real? I've loved you since the first time I saw you. God is so good. You are everything I want and need. The last one read pop me. Is he asking me to pop his virginity?

He read my mind, smiled, and he said the balloon Mila. I smiled with my back turned. The robe slipped me back into my little ensemble. I decided to pop the last balloon with the steak knife, it threw something at me. I stepped back startled but Samuel was entertained. He laughed at me so hard that my feelings were a little bit hurt, just a little bit. I looked to see what that was that the balloon threw at me. On the floor was a light purple princess cut diamond ring. I just stared at it for a minute. I picked it up to say no but when I turned around he was gone. Samuel was gone. What in the land of life is going on right here right now? I sat on the floor staring at this beautiful 24 karat white gold ring. It was beautiful. The phone to the room rang. I just wanted some good straight to the point dick tonight. "Hello." I already know its Samuel. "If you live for me, I promise that I will lay down, and die for you. Say yes Mila." He hung up. I want to fight it but for better or worse, I want to have a home filled with the love, kids, a puppy, a couple of little bunny rabbits, and laughs of family. I almost waved my flag to love but just like the now executed priest I want to die in love and even if it ends up being the wrong choice, I put the ring on. I agreed to be Mrs. Samuel Franklin. As quick as Samuel disappeared, he reappeared.

This is so amazing. I have never seen anything so beautiful looking at the now popped balloon that held the ring. I need this man right here right now. I am about to break him off like he is my first time. Samuel came back with a cellphone and played kissing on my tattoos by August Alsina. He said that the song and the phone are for me. I am not an iPhone fan but thanked him with a passionate kiss. I looked at his Rolex shining and pulled his shirt up over his head to start the meeting in this hotel room. I can feel my walls wanting to be filled with every inch of his dick. I hope it's thick. Layton says those are the best. I inhaled his cologne and exhaled my sensual desire. I do not mind spending my life with him at all but tonight, I am going to cease this moment and pretend that it's my birthday by making all of my dreams come true.

At this point, all I want to do is cum repeatedly. I instructed him to undress. Noticing that he was a little shy, I took it upon myself to turn around, and remove my ensemble before I laid back on the bed with my legs open. I wanted to skip the foreplay and get right down to business but he decided to rub both of my legs. Keep on and I'm going to fall asleep. I remember thinking until his lips started to kiss my legs from my ankles to my thighs then surprise, Samuel buried his head in between my legs and licked as though someone was going to take me from him. He sat back on his knees and looked at me trembling with satisfaction. I need more. I want more, so much more.

I reached for his dick to guide it in. Where is the base? Oh my God, it has no ending. I played with where it began and it was so thick that when he put it in me, I could not breathe. It felt so good that it hurt. The pain and pleasure together made me gasp for my next breath. I hope that he brought a back brace. I can't believe the first time with Damien just flashed before my eyes and I'm glad Samuel isn't reaching for a condom. I think he is too big for a condom. This is sweet. I found myself thanking the Lord he was all the way in until my heart ended up in my right shoulder to make room for this big black dick that he was equipped with. He had me yelling, "Ahhh, Samuel. Baby, baby, calm down." But it was too late, he was hard as rock, and ready for me. I can't let his first time be me screaming because it hurt memory. This man was everything and I do mean everything. "Fuck this." I whispered into his left ear before using my well-toned legs to wrap around his waist securing him to turn him on his back. I felt myself reach the point of no return the minute that I was on top of him. "Jesus loves me!" I screamed out with so much passion that it felt like the world shook. A virgin just turned me on to game.

Maybe they meant it in a different way, but it's true what they said about boyfriend number two, because he sure does know exactly what to do.

He is about to have me sitting on his lap and calling him big Daddy for the rest of the days no scratch that for all the days of his natural born life. The whole hotel including the guests, staff, and passer Byers are all about to know how we moving tonight and if they really don't, in a minute they will. I took in a breath to match each centimeter of that dick. This ride don't come with no seatbelts and I'm about to put this ass in reverse. We about to go to levels that will have him showing this entire hotel staff why he got to hit Mila, baby. "Okay Daddy, if this you want, then say you want it now?" Licking those lips, he looked me straight in my face and said, "Bitch, I already got it." Oh my God! Talk about showing somebody something this nigga caused my insides to throb from a deep pool of water to a mutha fuckan waterfall. He caused water to fall with so much passion all I could say was, "Jesus. Samuel." He reached into my soul and brought a little bitch called Slut up out of me. I rocked my body back and forth so hard that he had to pace himself not to cum. He grabbed my neck and kissed me hard but I wasn't feeling him being in control anymore.

"Nah, Nigga. Not tonight." I said before using my right hand to push his right hand away while pacing myself to face away from him. I tilted my head back allowing my reddish brown hair to send my sins flowing from inside of me. He just turned me from sweet little Mila to his personal trainer. "You better take this good stuff." He made a roaring sound and clapped back, "bitch you better give me this ass. Is this my pussy bitch?" Oh good God, why did he say that to me? I got my last nut out then pulled an aerobatic stunt that landed me on my side, feet to his head, "What you say big Daddy?" He took my tongue exploring his dick with only moans of approval. I let my hands work his dick in a jerking motion letting all that pre-cum slide right back out my mouth. I watched his balls get wet between me slobbering his dick down and all that pre-cum making its way down his dick. "I'm in love." Was all I heard before I started twisting my head back and forth ensuring that he know that I have all this Dick on lock.

Hands or no hands, he is all mine. This right here shows him that I don't have to be able to touch him to reach him. Mmmmmm, I moaned as though this big black dick was some sweet caramel. Grabbing his dick I stroke it to catch my breath. I looked at him, head tilted, and whisper, "fuck me." He smiles and sensually says, "I'm not here to talk." His left hand begins to play with my clit, which makes me even wetter. I wanted to watch him cum but he wasn't having that. Samuel grabs my waist at some point during my eyes being closed. Before I know it, I'm on my back getting my soul fucked out of my body. This dick is great. Our bodies start up a round of applause, but I love it too much so I scream, "Harder." He picked up his pace then picked me up like I weighed nothing to turn me over. I'm now on all fours where he can watch my thick ass bounce to his rhythm. Samuel's dick is throbbing inside of me. He fucks me harder asking, "Is this what you want? You my bitch? You like sucking your dick?" He turned me on and I wanted him more and more. He couldn't go any deeper but I wished for it anyway then just like that I came all over him. Samuel slowed down, rubbed my ass, then started that round of applause back up from our bodies hitting before his body starts to quiver into his point of no return. Nigga ain't a virgin no more. I felt him flood my insides and relax.

I looked over to the light from my new phone recording us and thought my first sex tape. We both on their putting it down, my eyes stayed low, and tonight I know my work going to keep him on the lock he asked for. There will never be a time that he wants to be anywhere that I'm not. Left hand on my ass, right hand on my back, he pulls his dick gently from me, "Dayuum, baby. I moaned before allowing my body to relax into the bed. It was cold and wet, but I didn't care. I screamed for air to breath between orgasms and here we are with him holding all the power he needs to own my thoughts. Samuel laid next to me, pulled me close, and let out a soft snore. It was cute. I relaxed the next few hours thinking about that amazing dick and delicious looking dinner I never got to eat. I'm hungry. Samuel was gone again. Talk about feeling stupid. I agreed to marry him, I let him have me without papers, and here we are with me and the beautiful ring. I inhaled my sins, sat up; put my robe on to go to the shower noticing a dress hung up for me to wear. It's beautiful, just my size. A letter was taped beside it, "Mila, last night was everything I dreamed of plus more. Your future will be full of love and no lies. Eternally Yours, Dr. Do Good." My face and heart lit up. My shower felt like a baptism, the soap unexpectedly nice, some sort of lavender scent. I know I was in there until the water got cold but I had no idea that Samuel was waiting on me next door, none at all.

Chapter Four

Lay your life on my path

      I returned to my room hungry but it wasn't empty. An African American couple sat in the loveseat happily in love. The man stood up to offer an introduction with his arms open. What the hell, I thought before Samuel came in behind me, "Right now, we can go get a marriage license then be off to get married, off to start our new life together as husband and wife. I know that his parents are dead so the first question on my mind is who are they? Reading my mind, Samuel introduced the couple as a preacher and his wife explaining they can make me his wife here and now. I agreed.

***

Happily Ever After

It was nice being Mila Franklin. I love being married. It's beautiful. I'm pregnant for the first time with twins and as scary as it is, it's also beautiful. My whole life is beautiful. Samuel and I got married in the hotel and spent our honeymoon there too at my request. It was amazing having food, massages, flowers, candy, and room service delivered to me daily. It's hard to believe that six months has gone by so fast. I'm getting the best of both worlds. I'm having a boy and a girl. We haven't chosen names yet but I do know I'm not making my son Franklin as the good doctor would like me to, No way and no how.

I know that my son will be handsome and my daughter will be beautiful. I'm not even upset that I'll never be a physician assistant. After a long talk with my Franklin, I'm going to be a stay at home mother. I am looking forward to that. I love my family so much that I simply don't want to miss a moment. Clearly, Franklin has to keep working, and he has no complaints about that. We agreed to never argue, nobody wins when family's feud anyway.

Layton and I became the best of friends. She is too funny and I get to live my life through her crazy adventures. I love hearing her sing. My husband has published all of her books and the thought of them going behind my back never crosses my mind. She is more like a sister than anything else to me. I can't see my finger looking feet anymore so she paints my toenails for me. Layton is brave. I never enjoyed getting to close to my own feet. She even agreed to be the Godmother.

Despite my pregnancy, Samuel stays licking from my neck to my navel. The OBGYN doctor said that all the sex we have should make delivery easier. Layton said, "Not if y'all rip her tummy open." She sure know a how to screw up a wet dream but in the same token though, she is the type to find the nearest mud puddle after the rain and make sure that you enjoy yourself. I'm going to miss her like crazy when she goes off to serve as an Army nurse. She said I took the last good man standing in Virginia so she is going to go find one sitting on the table injured. She said she needs a soldier who can cry. Layton is crazy for real. Don't anybody want a bitch boy, at least not me.

It's nice to have a man who shows me from morning to night how much he loves me. It's sweet to see him show me without ceasing how much he loves me. It's nice to have so much respect and loyalty, to get in all that I'm putting out and then some. It's even nicer to be able to live in a real life love story. I was told to slow things down but I didn't and now I'm happily married. The love of my life isn't your average story but it's mine. I can't wait to show the kids all of our videos and exchange of videos but I refuse for them to ever see the intimate parts. The minute my husband leaves, I cannot wait until he returns. My legs spread at the sound of him breathing. He saved my life, he saved my soul, and he introduced me to myself. The good Lord revealed what Damien's truth was and sent me my Boaz. I can honestly say that I have my happily ever after.

Made in the USA
Columbia, SC
26 June 2023